T0196876

Everlasting GRACE

S. M. WALKINGTON

BALBOA.
PRESS

A DIVISION OF HAY HOUSE

Balboa Press books may be ordered through booksellers or by contacting:

Balboa Press
A Division of Hay House
1663 Liberty Drive
Bloomington, IN 47403
www.balboapress.com.au
1 (877) 407-4847

Because of the dynamic nature of the Internet, any web addresses or
links contained in this book may have changed since publication and
may no longer be valid. The views expressed in this work are solely those
of the author and do not necessarily reflect the views of the publisher,
and the publisher hereby disclaims any responsibility for them.

The author of this book does not dispense medical advice or prescribe the use
of any technique as a form of treatment for physical, emotional, or medical
problems without the advice of a physician, either directly or indirectly. The
intent of the author is only to offer information of a general nature to help
you in your quest for emotional and spiritual well-being. In the event you use
any of the information in this book for yourself, which is your constitutional
right, the author and the publisher assume no responsibility for your actions.

Any people depicted in stock imagery provided by Thinkstock are
models, and such images are being used for illustrative purposes only.
Certain stock imagery © Thinkstock.

Print information available on the last page.

ISBN: 978-1-5043-1153-3 (sc)
ISBN: 978-1-5043-1154-0 (e)

Balboa Press rev. date: 11/27/2017

There are many people that have helped me with this book, and I would like to take this opportunity to thank them. To my mother, Astrid; my stepmother, Chantay; and my mother-in-law, Sue, thank you for your feedback. To my friends Lisa, Megan, Sam, Samara, Samantha, Cliff, Sara, and Jaimee, thank you for putting up with my badgering. And to my husband, Simon, thank you for putting up with all my ideas.

CHAPTER 1

1564—York, England

It was a cool spring night, and the air was thick with the sound of music and laughter. Old Master Gifford's new wife had given birth to a male heir last month, and that called for a celebration. All the gentry were in attendance, and Master Gifford had spared no expense. He had hired the best singers, dancers, and musicians he could find. There was even enough food to feed all the poor in York for days. As far as anyone could recall, Master Gifford had never held such an extravagant event for any of his six daughters. They had all been birthed by his first wife, who'd died on the birthing bed two years prior. He'd been remarried for only a year when his much younger second wife produced him a son. It was such a joy to watch the fair-haired, chubby babe being passed between his glowing dark-haired parents.

Master Gifford's happiness was to be celebrated by a masquerade ball. That's how Grace Heydon ended up there. Her father, Abraham Heydon, and Master Gifford were both wealthy landowners and long-time friends, so they were bound to attend. Grace's twelve-year-old sister, Marion, had to stay back at their estate, as their father deemed her too young to be out amongst society so late. But it wasn't just to celebrate young Arthur Gifford's birth that brought Grace here. There was also the promise of seeing Leonardo Stoke. Leonardo was the handsome son of another wealthy landowner, and Grace's father hoped they might marry so that his and Master Stokes's lands might be joined. Being the elder of two girls, it was Grace's responsibility to look and act her best to ensure her marriage was a good match, not only for her but also—and more importantly—for her family. Grace's mother had also died giving birth to a son, who unfortunately had died shortly after. Master Heydon couldn't bear to remarry, so he made sure his daughters were brought up proper and would marry well.

Grace sat on a bench, admiring all the guests in their fine clothes and exquisite masks. Most of the gentry, including her father, bought silk and other fine materials from the same merchant. He travelled the world, finding the best fabrics to sell to his customers. And he was well paid for it. All the guests proudly showed off his wares, each trying to outshine another.

Grace was keeping an eye out for a man wearing a green-and-blue mask with "A feather that would stand out." That's what Leonardo told her after the church service last Sunday. He had come up to her and told her he would be attending the ball and to look for him. So look for him she did.

It took a long time to prepare for this event, and Grace hoped she'd make a good impression. She was wearing a sky-blue full gown with a square neckline to show off her new gold necklace with a ruby pendant her father had given her for her recent twenty-first birthday. Under her decorated bodice was a corset, strung tight to give her the perfect shape. The forepart of her gown was light green and embroidered with beautiful flowers. Her sleeves were trumpeted, and the undersleeve was of the same material and colour as the forepart but left plain. Her brown eyes looked from behind a blue half mask held on by ribbon and decorated in precious stones. A dyed purple feather was a last-minute addition in hopes she would match Leonardo's mask. Her long, dark brown hair was curled and mostly hung loose down her back, as was the fashion of unwed ladies. The sides and front of her hair were held back with hairpins so her hair wouldn't get in her face.

Grace had her gaze trained on the entrance when a man walked in wearing a full-faced green-and-blue mask adorned with a large, beautiful peacock feather. The man wore a simple white jerkin under a black doublet and black boot hose with black boots. If she hadn't looked out for that particular mask, she wouldn't have looked twice at the man, but she was sure it was Leonardo. Although his clothes were not as colourful as others, they were made from quite expensive material. She watched the man look around the room, and then his gaze fixed on Grace. The man in the mask walked towards her. It seemed as if the crowd parted just for him. Grace sat up straighter and concentrated on her breathing, hoping it would settle her nerves. She had never had anything more than a polite conversation with Leonardo after church or at a social event, yet here she was, hoping for a dance. He stopped in front of her, bowed elegantly, and extended his hand. His mask looked her straight in the eyes. Grace reached up confidently, accepted his hand, and rose to her feet. The masked man led her through the other dancers to a vacant spot and turned her to face him. Grace placed her hand on his shoulder, and he put his hand on her waist.

From this ready position, the masked man led them in dance. He was a very good dancer and moved swiftly with sure feet. Grace was thankful for all the dance lessons her father had put her through; she was able to keep up quite well. As they moved and twirled across the dance floor, Grace tried to make out the features behind the mask. He had the same build and dark hair as Leonardo. But she couldn't view the eyes, as they were hidden behind a mesh in the mask. The mask itself looked fine. Up close, Grace could see that even though the colours were simple, the feather made it stunning.

Grace was really enjoying herself, but after a few turns, she started to feel hot and out of breath. Her corset suddenly felt too tight, and the room too crowded. She leaned in close and whispered to the masked man, "Sir, 'tis overwarm in here. Would you be so kind as to accompany me outside?"

The silent masked man nodded, held out his arm for her to grab onto, and led them outside to a small balcony. They were all alone, giving Grace the perfect opportunity to talk to the gentleman. The burning desire to see Leonardo's face was overwhelming, so Grace stood in front of him and took off her mask so he could see her face. She felt the masked man's eyes going over her and prayed that he liked what he saw. To settle the butterflies in her stomach, Grace took as big a breath as her corset would allow her. "Now let's see whose face is behind *this* mask," said Grace. Standing on her tiptoes, she reached up boldly and grabbed the straps that held the mask in place. The man momentarily grabbed her wrists, but Grace said, "It's okay; I want to know who you are," and she lifted the mask gently off his face.

Grace didn't mean to gasp out loud. She was just surprised—very surprised. For underneath that mask was not Leonardo, as she had thought it may have been, but the merchant everyone bought their fabrics from. *No wonder he is so well dressed,* Grace thought. *Master Gifford must have invited him as a thank-you for all the fabrics he brought back for his daughters.*

The disappointment must have shown on Grace's face, for the merchant said in a deep voice, "What's wrong, fair lady?"

Not daring to look him in the eye, as Grace was embarrassed and felt stupid for the mistaken identity, she replied, "I am sorry. You are not who I thought you were."

"Who was I meant to be?" the merchant asked, brushing a stray bit of hair away from her face. Grace looked up at him and studied his features. He was handsome in the way of an older gentleman. He had black hair like Leonardo, but he had green eyes that didn't look as kind.

"Someone else," she replied, and she moved to put her mask on.

As she was bringing the mask back up to her face, he reached out and grabbed her arm. "Such beauty should not be hidden behind a mask. Stay out here with me, and let us talk some more."

"I really must go," Grace replied, trying to pull her arm out of his grasp. As his grip tightened, Grace started to panic. "Please let me go. I am expected inside!"

His eyes bore into hers, and with one last tight squeeze, he released his grip. His mouth turned into a polite smile that did not extend up to his eyes. "But of course. Please forgive me." He stepped back, allowing Grace to pass.

Grace walked past him as fast as she could and went back into the ballroom, desperate to get back among the other guests. She could feel his eyes on her as she walked away.

Grace found a bench near a group of people. She sat down and composed herself. Thinking over it, Grace felt cheated and irritated. The man she had been dancing with was in fact just a merchant. He must have learned what Leonardo was wearing and worn the same to trick Grace into a dance. He had commented once that she looked beautiful, but she had assumed that was because she was wearing some fabrics he had sold her father. Grace was so busy fuming over the merchant stealing a dance that she didn't notice a man had sat down next to her.

"Good evening, my lady. What seems to have your attention?" he asked.

Startled, Grace looked up at the man, who wore a blue-and-green mask with a white feather. It wasn't as big and beautiful as the peacock feather, but it still looked nice. "Leonardo? Is that you?" she asked, hoping it was.

"Indeed it is. Were you expecting someone else?" he replied with amusement in his voice.

"No. Just ensuring that is you I am speaking to. All these masks, and you cannot be sure who is behind them."

"Too true!" Leonardo laughed. "Any of these people could be a servant dressed up."

Or a merchant, Grace thought to herself. She looked across the room and saw that the masked merchant was leaning against a wall, watching her, and she felt a shiver go through her.

"Are you cold? Let us dance; that will warm you up!" said Leonardo, taking her hand.

Determined to put the awful encounter with the merchant behind her, Grace was the first to get up off the bench. Leonardo took her hand and walked them onto the dance floor, joining the other dancers. Leonardo led them gracefully around the dance floor. As they were moving around, Grace kept an eye out for the merchant. For some reason, she didn't want him watching them. When she was certain she couldn't see him any more, she let herself relax. *This moment is for you and Leonardo,* Grace thought to herself. *Don't let horrible men ruin this for you.*

Leonardo and Grace spent the night dancing, laughing and talking together. Not once did they leave each other's side. Once during the night, they were talking to Grace's father, and he remarked how wonderful they looked together. At that point, Leonardo looked her in the eye and said, "I couldn't agree more, sir."

Upon hearing that, Grace felt a glow from within her chest. "I am glad you think so, Leonardo," Grace answered. It seemed she had made a good impression after all.

At the end of the night, Leonardo walked her and her father to their awaiting coach. Grace stopped outside the coach and allowed her father to go inside first so she could say goodbye to Leonardo without him watching. She faced Leonardo, who took her hand in his, lifted it to his mouth, and laid a kiss on it. "Thank you for a wonderful evening," he said.

"The pleasure was all mine!" breathed Grace.

"Hopefully I shall see you soon?" asked Leonardo.

"I would like that," replied Grace, and he helped her into the coach. When she sat down, her father had the most delighted look on his face. Grace couldn't help but mirror his delight.

The next day, Grace was sitting in the garden, enjoying the rare bit of sunshine that peeked through the clouds. She was reminiscing about the night before with Leonardo when she saw a coach pull up to her father's estate. With great anticipation, she watched it travel up the driveway and stop outside the front steps. From where she was sitting, she could see quite well who got out of that coach. It was Mr. Stokes, followed closely by his son Leonardo. A radiant smile appeared on Grace's face, and she watched as one of the servants greeted them and then led them inside. Minutes passed, and Grace's younger sister, Marion, came running out of the door and over to Grace.

"Grace, Grace!" she yelled, running over excitedly, "they are talking about you!"

Grace, trying to be the older role model, said, "Now calm down, Marion; running about and spying is no way for a young lady to act. I am sure if they are talking about me, they will tell me all I need to know when I need to know. Now walk back inside for your lessons."

"I was not spying!" Marion said. She pouted and tried to argue the point, but Grace made her go back to the estate. Grace was feeling really excited. She hoped that they would finish their talks so she could go and ask her father about their visit—even if it was unladylike.

Moments later, Leonardo came walking out of the estate

and started towards her in a confident stride. Grace quickly adjusted her dress so it sat neatly and watched him approach with great eagerness.

"Good afternoon, Leonardo. How fare you?" she asked.

"I am well, sweet Grace, and how are you?" he replied, bowing.

"I am well also. I thought it such a beautiful day that I would spend it out in the garden."

"What a beautiful garden it is. Please, let us walk and admire it," Leonardo said, holding out his arm for her. Grace accepted his arm, and they started to walk along the paths. After they had walked a few feet, Leonardo cleared his throat and said, "My father and I just had an interesting conversation with your father."

"Oh?" replied Grace, who instantly felt stupid at her short reply.

"Yes. Our fathers seem to think that it will be mutually beneficial to them if we wed."

"Oh!" Grace replied again, wishing she could find other words to use.

"And I happen to agree," Leonardo went on. He didn't seem put off by her lack of words. "What do you think, fair Grace?"

"I-I agree also," Grace stammered out.

"Then it is settled. We shall tell our fathers the happy news, and we shall be wed before summer starts!"

"Of course," said Grace. She couldn't believe it was happening. All she had ever wanted to do was make her father proud, and that meant becoming a wife and bearing her husband many children, and she would get to do that with none other than Leonardo! There was only a month left of spring, and there was so much to organize. Leonardo reached into his pocket and pulled out a beautiful ring with a ruby on it and put it on Grace's right hand.

"I know how much you like rubies," Leonardo said. "I got it to match your beautiful necklace."

Leonardo and Grace walked down to the house arm in arm and told their fathers the good news. Their fathers were both delighted and proceeded straight into planning the wedding. Grace sat herself down on a chair to steady herself; all the excitement had made her feel light-headed. She watched the three grown men talk wedding plans—especially the one that was going to be her husband. He was very animated and very sure on what he wanted. Not one of the men asked Grace what she wanted, but she didn't mind. They could have got married in the kitchen for all it mattered to her, as long as Leonardo was there. Grace also spent a lot of time admiring the ring that Leonardo had given her. It was beautiful, and it did indeed match her necklace perfectly. She decided that she would wear them both proudly from now on. That way everyone would know that Leonardo loved her.

It was about an hour later when their guests departed. Leonardo and Grace were to be wed in four weeks' time at the local church that both of the families attended. This gave enough time for the announcement at church over the next few Sundays to make sure everyone was happy with their arrangement. Grace couldn't see why anyone would have a problem with their union. They were perfectly matched in every way. Leonardo's father was giving them one of his properties so that they would have somewhere to live after they had wed, and Grace's father was already sorting the finances for the wedding. After the wedding, they would all go to Master Stokes's estate for an extravagant after-wedding feast. Grace was full of excitement. She was looking forward to being Leonardo's wife and having his children.

That night, Grace could hardly sleep. She was so happy yet so nervous. Her life was about to change in a big way. Grace kept looking at her new ruby ring with a big smile on her face, her head swimming with plans for their future together.

Two days later, Grace was summoned by her father to the sitting room. As she walked in, she saw her father talking to a man. She couldn't see who it was, as both of the men had their backs to her. They were examining something laid out on a table.

"… needs to be the best you have got," her father was instructing the man.

"I have the exact fabric you are looking for," replied the man.

The men must have sensed Grace enter the room, as both of them turned around and looked at her. Her father greeted her with a warm smile, whereas the man had only a cold stare. Grace felt fear deep in her stomach, for it was the merchant standing next to her Father. He must have been invited so they could purchase some fabric for Grace's gown.

"Good morning, Grace; have you met Solomon Vinter?" her father said, gesturing to the merchant. "He is the man that brings us all the beautiful fabrics you like to wear."

"Good morning, Father; I have seen him here a few times but have never been formally introduced," she replied, trying to keep herself composed. The merchant's glare was making her feel uneasy. It was as if his stare were piercing right through her.

"You see, Solomon, my Grace is getting married to young Leonardo Stoke soon, and she deserves the best there is!" her father boasted proudly.

"Well, congratulations, my lady," Solomon said while bowing, still not breaking his stare. "I know exactly what you deserve."

Solomon walked over to Grace's father, leaned in close, and whispered something Grace couldn't hear in his ear. Mr. Heydon's face went blank, and his eyes went unfocused. He then walked out of the room and closed the door behind him as if he were in a trance. Grace watched with her mouth open. Her father would never leave her alone in a room with a stranger. Ignoring Solomon, she walked over to the door to find that it was locked. Feeling breath on her neck, Grace turned around, and Solomon was standing right behind her with a dark look on his face.

"So, Grace, you are getting married? To that boy Leonardo? I'll give you a chance to change your mind. I have been watching you for a long time now, and you deserve much better. You will only be something he can show off when he is not with his whores. You will be used for childbirth and for your father's lands. Marry me and I will give you the world. Marry me and you won't be for show!"

Anger started to overtake the fear, and Grace mustered up all the courage she could find. "You are a merchant," she said, "just a merchant, and Leonardo is from a good family, and he loves me. I will not lower myself or my family to wed you. Your actions disgust me, and I must ask you to leave this estate!"

Grace was breathing heavily now, and she watched the merchant carefully. She didn't dare turn her back on him, so she put her hands behind her and started to wiggle the door handle in hopes it would swing open, but she found it was still locked.

"Well," he sneered, "I wish you a long and happy life then!"

Solomon's hands moved quicker than Grace's eyes could see as he reached up and ripped the ruby necklace that hung from her neck in one swift movement. Shocked, Grace reached up to the spot where the pendant had been touching her skin. With his other hand, he grabbed Grace around the throat and pushed her hard up against the door. Grace's vision had stars come across it, and her head started to ache from hitting the door so hard. Trying to fight back, Grace brought one hand up to his hand at her throat, and with the other she tried to scratch at Solomon's face, hoping to inflict enough damage to cause him to release her. Solomon swatted her hands away as if they were nothing, grabbed some of Grace's hair, and pulled it out, roots and all. Tears sprang to Grace's eyes as she tried desperately to cry out, but his grip on her throat was too strong. After he pocketed her precious necklace and hair, he pulled out a small dagger and a small vial. Seeing the blade, Grace started to panic and kicked feebly at his leg. He forced himself closer to her so her legs were pinned between his and the door. Grace felt sickened by the close contact and tried to fight back harder. He then raised the dagger, brought it up to Grace's cheek, and made a cut. Grace felt the blade pierce her and froze in fear. Solomon then used the vial to collect some of her blood. Grace's heart was pounding in her chest; she was certain he was going to finish her off. Amidst all the wrestling and tears, all she could think of was her beloved Leonardo and the life they could have had.

As quickly as the attack started, the merchant stepped away from Grace, letting her fall forward onto the ground in a heap. As soon as she drew in a proper breath, she started to cough uncontrollably, making her throat feel worse. Solomon looked down at her with such contempt; she thought he was going to kick her and tried to brace herself for the impact. Instead he just moved her out of the way with his foot and went out of the door. A moment later, Grace heard the front door open and close. Grace started to shake and cry uncontrollably when she realized she was safe. Her head was hurting from hitting the door, and her throat was sore from Solomon's grip and from coughing so much. She heard footsteps come thundering in and saw her father's shoes come into her vision.

"What is the meaning of this?" her father asked. Grace felt his hands on her as he helped her to her feet. He gasped loudly when he saw that there was a cut on her cheek "Did that merchant do this you?" he demanded, touching her cheek. All Grace could do was nod. Her throat was too sore to talk, and she didn't think she could stop crying long enough to speak.

"I don't know what came over me," her father said with remorse. "I should never left you alone with him. Stay here; I shall gather some men, and we shall see to him." He moved Grace to a seat and then went and got one of the servants to help clean her up. "See to Mistress Grace's needs and make sure that cut doesn't leave a mark on her face. She is to be married soon!" her father said before leaving the room.

Grace sat in that chair most of the night, waiting for her father to come home and replaying the awful attack over in her head. She couldn't believe the vile things that had come out of the merchant's mouth! Leonardo was a gentleman and would never hurt her, unlike Solomon. They were going to have a long and happy life together filled with love and children. Whilst waiting for her father's return, the strangest thing happened to her. She heard someone whispering but couldn't tell where from. She looked around the room to try to find the source, but it got so loud it filled the whole room. Also, her heartbeat quickened, and a tingling sensation spread throughout her whole body; then her skin started to glow. Her body was glowing so much it illuminated the whole room around her. At the same time, her vision went all red and blurry. Trying not to panic, she blinked and rubbed her eyes to try to clear her vision, and within moments everything went back to normal. The glowing stopped, her vision cleared, and the whispering ceased. Grace sat still for a few moments to make sure everything was as it should be. "I must have imagined it," Grace mumbled to herself, praying she wasn't going mad.

It was a few hours later when her father returned with Leonardo. Grace was so relieved to see him come through the door. She got up to greet them, and Leonardo embraced her tightly and then looked at her face. "Are you all right, my dear? Our men are out hunting him as we speak. We shall avenge this outrage!"

Grace's heart sank. They hadn't found him. How was she to feel safe again? Grace's father came up to her and said, "I rounded up all the men I could find, but we couldn't find him. We went to his residence, broke down the door, and searched the whole house from top to bottom, and still no sign of him," Grace's father took a deep breath and looked at her gravely. "While searching, we did come upon some curious items. We believe them to be items that belong to a sorcerer!"

Hearing that made Grace feel weak in the knees, and she had to sit back down again. With fear in her heart, she remembered what had happened to her earlier. *Please, God, let me not be cursed!*

CHAPTER 2

Present time, San Francisco

Grace sat behind the wheel of her Jeep and watched the funeral procession drive through the traffic lights she was stopped at. Feeling jealous of the body inside of the hearse was not a normal human emotion, but then again, it had been a while since Grace had felt like a normal human. The light changed to green, and Grace continued on to the airport, where she was to meet her long-time friend and housemate, Rose Turner. Rose was a witch Grace had helped during the persecution of witches when she was living in Connecticut in 1692. Since then, Rose had vowed to help Grace end her curse or track down the sorcerer behind it. In order to do that, Rose had to become immortal too. It seemed the curse Solomon had cast was a very powerful one, and hunting for one man with immense power takes a few centuries. It took a few years of searching for an immortality spell for Rose, but they finally found one through a warlock. He was also hiding from the witch hunts. When Rose told him that Grace had risked her life and had saved her, he gave her a spell to freeze her age. The only condition was that she had to do a ritual during the full moon once a year to keep the spell going. Well, that is what Rose told her anyhow. Grace was quite wary of magic, so she didn't ask too many questions.

Rose had been over in Europe, chasing a hopeful lead into Solomon's location. Grace couldn't go where Rose was going—secret witches' business and all—so she stayed behind and worked. They were not in immediate need of money, but working helped to keep them busy. When you work for centuries and make good investments, you tend to build up quite a good nest egg. At the moment, Grace and Rose owned and ran a florist. It was a lovely little corner shop that had two other employees to help with arrangements and deliveries. It brought great joy to Grace to see her customers leave with a beautiful bouquet of flowers, or a child bury his or her face in a flower to get a good smell. She had developed the knack of knowing exactly what the customer was after. Whether it was an "I love you," or a "Congratulations!" Grace made sure everyone left happy. Over the many years, Grace had been a librarian, a receptionist at a law firm, a bank teller, and even a dog walker. Rose had worked as a tour guide, a receptionist at an opposing law firm, an antiques dealer, and once even a teacher. They had had a lot of time to get professions, but they could work in them for only a little while. According to Rose's teaching papers, she should be nearing sixty years old, so she couldn't use them any more. Grace had also studied nursing, but she had decided not to work as a nurse. She didn't think she could handle seeing so much life and death in one spot when she herself couldn't experience either.

Pulling up to the pickup point, Grace spotted Rose

straight away. She was hard to miss with her dark skin, long black hair, brown eyes, and the best smile anyone could have. She was frantically waving her hand around to get Grace's attention—not that she needed to; she was wearing white jeans and a yellow-and-orange top. Rose loved colours and liked to be as bright as she could when she went out. Her colourful outfits were always turning heads, even if they were not intended to. Grace was more conservative. She preferred jeans and darker colours like reds, blues, and blacks. She kept her hair mid-length these days, as it was easiest to handle, and generally wore simple makeup. She wore just enough makeup to hide the scar on her cheek. Grace pulled to a stop right in front of Rose and waited for her to put her bags in the back of the Jeep and get in. Once Rose got in, Grace took off again and headed back to their flat.

"So how was the trip?" Grace asked. She missed her friend dearly and wanted to know everything.

"Fantastic! Europe has changed so much since we were last there. I brought you back some books you will love!"

The last time they went back to Europe was back in the 1900s. They had heard Solomon was there and went looking but came up empty-handed.

"Thanks, my book room needed a few more," replied Grace. In their four-bedroom flat, there was one room dedicated to Grace's books. She loved to collect and read books and had plenty of time to do it. Rose used the other spare bedroom for her witchcraft. Grace avoided that room if she could. All the magical objects, crystals, and jars holding various items in there made Grace feel uneasy.

"You're welcome. That's not all I brought back, though. I got some information about your sorcerer."

"Is it better than the last lot of information you got?" Grace hoped it was. The most recent bit of information they had received was that he was living in Australia. As it turned out, it was just a man with the same name that was known to be a local pest.

"It most definitely is. The name you know him by isn't his actual name. He has been changing his name over the years to help him fit in. Just like us."

This was true. On paper, Grace was known as Cindy Lane and Rose was known as Renee Phelp. Every twenty years or so, they had to change their identities and move to different towns; otherwise, people would question them on how they stayed young. One time, Grace was in a bad mood and replied to one of them with "Piss off a sorcerer and get him to curse you." That was followed by laughs and her co-worker asking her where to find one. If only Grace knew.

"I thought that might have been the case," replied Grace. "Did you find out his actual name?"

"Well, no. Though there are whispers of a coven that knows all about him, but he nearly killed them all, so they have gone into hiding."

"Hiding," said Grace, feeling downhearted. "Does anyone know where they are?"

"There has been talk that they have been hiding in Europe. That's why I came back. I think we both need to go next time. I have a feeling that if we ever find this coven, they will want to meet the person who is so interested in Solomon."

Grace sighed. *Of course. Nothing to do with the sorcerer*

is ever simple. They didn't get many leads when it came to the sorcerer, so each one they got needed to be checked out.

Grace pulled into her designated parking spot and killed the engine. They both got out of the car, and Grace helped Rose take her luggage up to their flat. Rose then went to her room to unpack her bags, while Grace went to the kitchen to start tea. Grace stared at the pot of boiling spaghetti and thought about what Rose had told her. It had only been during the last century that they had been able to settle down and really start looking for Solomon, or whatever his name was. In the 1700s and 1800s it was very hard for two women to survive on their own. They still needed clothes, shelter, and food. Even though neither of them could die, being hungry and exposed to the elements hurt, and they both could still feel pain all right. Grace remembered the pain of hunger too well; that was why she didn't think twice when it came to charities. They often donated bouquets for fundraisers—anonymously, of course, as they didn't like to attract attention.

Grace could hear her friend moving around in her room. She was so thankful she found Rose. Grace had hidden her in a tailor shop that she was working in as an embroiderer. Grace was taught by her maid when she was living with Leonardo. Not having any children had left Grace with a lot of time on her hands, so she decided to create things in a different way. Since she never needed to use the skill until she needed to provide for herself, she was slow in her work, but she was very good at it. Grace would endeavour to make sure her work was perfect. Grace convinced the owner to hire her by telling him that she was a widow whose husband died at sea and that she needed money to sail home to England to be with her family. It wasn't all a lie. Leonardo was long dead, but she actually needed the money for food and to help keep a roof over her head. All the money and jewels she had brought over with her from England did not last long after she arrived. Many people took advantage of a young woman on her own.

Grace was working late one night to catch up on work when a frightened-looking girl came running into the shop. Grace was the only one there, and she got a shock when a little girl came running through the shop door. Grace looked at the girl and noticed that her clothes were of simple material but were well made. She was covered in dirt and was panting as if she had just run a long way

"I'm sorry, but we are closed," Grace told the girl.

The girl looked at Grace with wide eyes as if she were going to get thrown out. She turned her head and looked nervously at the door. Grace heard a commotion happening outside and got up to look through the window. She saw a few people running around the streets, shouting as if they were looking for something or someone. Not liking the look of them, Grace turned to the frightened little girl, who looked up at Grace with tears streaming down her face. Grace felt so sorry for this girl. She knew what it was like to be frightened, so she listened to her instincts and hid the girl in the back room under a big pile of cloths that were waiting to be sorted. Grace locked the shop door and returned to her sewing and acted as if nothing had happened. A moment later, an angry-looking man peered through the shop window and banged on the door. Grace got up and went over to answer the pounding.

"Shop is closed!" she yelled through the door.

The man banged louder. "Open this door at once!" he yelled back at her.

He was hitting the door so hard that Grace was worried he was going to break it down. Grace opened the door and took a step back as he barged in.

"Have you seen a young girl?" asked the man, looking around the shop.

Grace instantly hated him. There was something about him that didn't sit right with Grace, and that included his hunting terrified little girls.

"No. There is no one here but me. I have had the shop locked all night and have only just opened the door to let you in," said Grace, keeping her voice steady.

A sceptical look came across the man's face, and Grace continued. "You are free to look around if you wish. Just don't make a mess of the place." She prayed that he wouldn't take her up on the offer. It looked as though he was about to when a much younger man put his head through the door.

"She has been spotted heading towards the woods!" The young man said, out of breath. The first man pushed through the store door, almost knocking the much younger man over. The younger man quickly righted his feet and followed after him.

After they had both left, Grace locked the shop door and extinguished all lights. She sat quiet for a while to make sure they had indeed gone. When she was sure, she went into the back room and uncovered the frightened-looking girl.

"It's okay," Grace told her. "They are gone now. You are safe."

The girl looked up at Grace and stared at her as if she were reading her.

"You have an old soul," said the little girl in a small voice.

Grace was slightly taken aback. "I am only twenty-one." That was the age she had been telling everyone since she had stopped ageing.

"You have been that age for a long time," the girl replied.

Grace could hardly believe her ears. How could this little girl know so much?

"How …?" Grace started to ask, but she found herself lost for words.

"They are chasing me because my family and I are witches. They have taken my mother from the family we worked for. My mother has the sight, and she saw them coming. She woke me up early and made me leave her so I could escape. I tried to go back to help her, but I got chased by a group of men." The sadness was thick in her voice, and it made Grace's heart ache.

Grace stood and thought for a moment. Even though she truly felt for the poor girl, she hoped she hadn't made a mistake by hiding her. The only other magical person she had met had cursed her, so she was quite wary.

"You do not need to fear me. I am not him. I can help you like you have helped me," she said while getting out of the basket she had hidden in.

Grace regarded the girl. She had kind eyes—the kind of eyes that one could trust. She had said she could help Grace, and Grace definitely needed help. She had been alive for 128 years now, and this young girl was the first person she had met that knew anything about the curse. She considered that maybe they were destined to meet.

"All right," said Grace, "but we can no longer stay here.

It won't be long before they come back here to look for you. I have some money I have been saving up that we can use to get far away from here. Tell me, child, what is your name?"

"My name is Rose Turner, ma'am," replied the girl, curtsying.

Rose, Just like my favourite flower, thought Grace

"Grace—please call me Grace."

Grace started to feel a bit anxious, as she now had to come up with a plan on how to escape the town without being seen. She looked at Rose and then at the rest of the shop. An idea came to her when her eyes fell upon a dress that was hanging up. *That would almost fit Rose*, Grace thought to herself. She went over to the dress and grabbed it off the rack. Grace then walked over to Rose and handed it to her.

"Quickly, go into the back room and get changed into this dress," Grace instructed. Rose reached out and accepted the dress. Her eyes grew big when she felt the rich fabric.

"It's okay. The tailor still owes me my week wage, and I will not be around to collect it," Grace said. Rose nodded and then disappeared into the back room. While she was in there, Grace picked out a dress that was still waiting to be collected. She had worked on this dress herself and was rather fond of her handiwork. Rose emerged several minutes later wearing the new dress with her old dress in hand. Even though the new dress was a bit too big, it looked stunning on her, as if it had been made just for her.

"Wait here a moment; I need to change too," said Grace as she went into the back room. She wasted no time in changing into the new robes. The dress was a bit tight, but she could put up with it for now. When she was done, she grabbed as much cloth as she could carry from the pile that Rose had been hiding in and returned to the front room. Rose was standing in the shadows, nervously looking towards the shop door.

"Here is what we are going to do. There is a river a few streets over. If we can leave through the back door without being seen, we can stuff these dresses with all this fabric and toss them into the river. By the time those horrid men realize I have hidden you, they will come looking for us. Hopefully someone will see the stuffed dresses and mistake them for our bodies. By the time they get the clothes out of the river, we will be long gone." Grace was quite proud of herself for thinking up such a plan so quickly.

"Yes, ma'—er, I mean Grace," said Rose.

"After we throw these in, we will go past the house I board at and collect my things. The older gentleman I live with will be asleep. He is nearly deaf, so there is no danger of us waking him."

Rose nodded, and they went to the rear exit of the shop. After Grace checked that the coast was clear, they headed out, moving as quickly and as quietly as they dared. Grace kept looking behind her to check on Rose. The poor dear was struggling to keep up, as she had to keep herself from tripping over her dress, but Grace dared not go any slower. It took a good half an hour to get to the river. Every now and then they would hear someone yell something from a few streets away, which made them stop moving for a few moments.

They finally got to the river and dumped the stuffed dresses. As they watched the decoys float down the river, Grace wondered if she would ever have to do something like this again. As soon as the floating masses of clothes disappeared from sight, Grace led Rose to the residence she was staying at. She was very lucky to have found a place to live. The old gentleman that lived there was in need of company, and Grace was in need of a place to stay. Even though he was poor of hearing, he enjoyed the company. Grace would often read aloud to him, even though she had to talk very loudly. Grace would miss him sorely, but this young girl was in need of help. If Grace didn't help Rose, she wouldn't be able to live with herself.

It didn't take Grace long to gather her few belongings. She decided against leaving a note; as much as it upset her not to say goodbye and thank you, she didn't want the old gentleman getting harassed by thugs. When she was ready to leave, she found Rose was standing in the doorway awkwardly.

"Everything is going to be all right, little Rose. We are going to find somewhere new to live, and I am going to look after you."

With that said, Grace took one last look at her former home, and they then both left to start a new life. From that night on, Grace kept to her word and looked after Rose. At times it was really tough for Grace; she didn't want to let Rose down. After being alone for so long, it was daunting to be responsible for somebody else. As Rose grew older and the years passed, Grace knew she had made the right decision that night.

Grace finished cooking tea and served it up. She then went and knocked on Rose's bedroom door.

"Tea's ready," yelled Grace, and she headed back to the table.

Rose came out of her room, sat down at the table, and fixed her gaze on Grace with a look Grace had come to know as Rose's "trouble face."

"What's up?" asked Grace, hoping that she wouldn't regret asking. The last time Rose had used a look like this, they had ended up in Northern Russia, looking for some plant Rose needed for a spell she was trying. The plant they came back with ended up getting confiscated by customs on return. Rose sulked for weeks.

"Well, I just had a phone call from a contact in Bulgaria. She needs help and has asked us for a favour," Rose said, seemingly picking her words carefully.

"And what is that?" replied Grace, starting to feel curious.

"They have been having a kind of an animal problem."

"Animal problem? Don't they have people that deal with animals there?" asked Grace

"Not for this kind of animal," said Rose as she put down her fork and looked at Grace. "It's a werewolf problem."

Grace stopped mid-chew and looked at Rose, waiting for a punchline. When Rose didn't drop one, Grace had to ask. "A werewolf? As in a human who transforms during a full moon?"

"And when they experience great emotions or have developed the self-control skills to transform at will," Rose said nonchalantly.

Grace thought this information over. "Are you joking?"

Rose sighed. "Grace, you are a four-hundred-fifty-two-year-old woman who cannot die who lives with a mighty powerful witch, even if I do say so myself, and you have trouble believing in werewolves?"

"Well you haven't brought them up before," said Grace.

"That's because it was thought that they had been hunted into extinction. Their venom and fur are needed for some very powerful spells, so some magical folk used to pay hunters to hunt them. Turns out there is at least one still around, and they may need help. They might not even know what's happening to them."

Upon hearing that, Grace knew she had to help. Not knowing what was going on with one's own body was something she could relate to. Discovering she was immortal had turned her life upside down.

"Okay. It is time we moved on anyway. We have been here eight years and gave it a good run." After thinking for a moment, Grace added, "I think we should sign the shop over to Kendra and Anna. They know how to run the shop, and they have always worked really hard." Kendra was a single mother who had never taken a sick day while working for them, and Anna was close on retiring but showed no signs of slowing down.

"Oh, I agree," replied Rose. "Those ladies have run the shop themselves many times so we could travel. They deserve it."

"Glad you agree. I'll speak to a solicitor about getting the paperwork sorted, and you can talk to your document guy about new identities," Grace said, getting up from the table. She had a lot to organize and needed to start right away.

"Sure. Got any preference for a name?" asked Rose.

"Surprise me," said Grace with a grin. New identities were always fun.

That night, Grace had trouble sleeping, so she decided to get on the net and start her research on werewolves. While she fired up her laptop, she went and got herself a hot chocolate and settled in. Grace logged on and opened up the internet browser. She typed in "werewolf," and waited for the search engine to load. It didn't take long, and there was a range of results from popular TV shows and movies to ancient lore. Grace decided to go with the ancient lore; she didn't think the movies got it right often. Grace clicked on a link a few pages in and proceeded to read the text.

> A werewolf (also known as a lycanthrope) is a human that has the ability to shapeshift into a wolf-like creature during the phase of the full moon. Werewolves can also shapeshift at will after they learn to control their curse. The werewolf curse is transmitted via the werewolf bite. If a person is bitten by a werewolf, that person will be infected with the curse and will start transforming during the next full moon. A werewolf is most vulnerable when in human form. Even when werewolves are in werewolf form, they are not immortal. Whilst they can die from mortally inflicted wounds by other weapons, silver weapons are the most effective as, silver also poisons

them. There is no known cure for the werewolf curse.

Grace reread the information and sat back in her seat. This was different to her usual routine. A week ago she was looking at flower arrangements online, and now she was looking up werewolves.

Grace printed the page off and got up from her desk. She left her room and knocked on Rose's bedroom door. When there was no answer, Grace opened the door a crack to see if she was in. A quick scan confirmed that Rose wasn't asleep in her bed, so Grace went down the hall to Rose's spell room. Grace took a deep breath and knocked on the door. Again there was no answer. Grace knew Rose was in there, but she was too apprehensive to go inside. Ever since her encounter with the sorcerer, Grace had trouble trusting magic.

CHAPTER 3

It was three weeks later when Rose and Grace finally left San Francisco under the aliases "Veronica," and "Lucy." The only people that had seen them off at the airport were the two employees that had worked for them at the florist. It was sad to leave them, but it was time. Grace tried not to make too many friends wherever they went. That's what she hated the most about this life: every relationship had an expiry date—no exceptions. This was a good reason why Grace didn't date. There was no future in it. Rose had encouraged her to give it a try, as she would on occasions go on a few dates, but Grace couldn't bring herself to. She was still feeling raw from Leonardo's betrayal. Even though it had happened centuries ago, she still got that hollow feeling in her chest when she thought back to their marriage.

About five hours into the flight, Grace's eyes were feeling tired from reading the book she had brought along, so she decided to try to sleep. Grace always had trouble sleeping on planes—not Rose, though; she was sleeping soundly next to her, as she had been for most of the trip. Grace checked the seat behind her and reclined it a bit, hoping not to disturb the person sitting behind her. The man behind her met her eyes and gave her a slight nod as if to say "Yeah, that's fine." Grace smiled politely back and turned back around to get comfortable. It took a bit of wriggling and rearranging herself to get comfortable, but she eventually drifted off into sleep.

Grace is walking along a stone path. She can't see her surroundings, as she is surrounded by a dense fog. She feels as if she needs to walk faster, as she needs to get to her destination as quickly as she can. Grace picks up the pace and starts to jog. Dread washes over her; she is worried she is going to be late. Running now, Grace runs through some open gates and stops. The fog lifts, and Grace sees that she has entered a graveyard. Why is she here? Grace has a feeling she knows where she has to go. She trusts her feet and lets them take her in the right direction. The further in Grace goes, the older the headstones appear to be. Grace's eyes lock on to a headstone a few rows away. "There," Grace says, and she starts to head towards it. Moving quickly now, Grace weaves through the other headstones, not really watching her footing. A few times she stumbles but manages to keep her footing. She is getting closer now, and her skin is tingling.

Grace jerked awake. The plane had hit some turbulence that disturbed her slumber. She rubbed her eyes and looked over at Rose, who was still fast asleep. *Wish I could sleep like that!* Grace thought to herself. She looked at her phone and noticed she had been asleep for only half an hour. Grace decided to use this time to go to the bathroom. Once there, she stood in the cubicle for a bit, examining her reflection.

She looked like she felt—tired. Grace returned to her seat with the intention of trying to go back to sleep, but when she sat down, she noticed that Rose had woken up.

"Good sleep?" asked Grace.

"Yeah," said Rose, stretching. "Did you manage to get some rest?"

"Yeah, I managed to get a few winks in," replied Grace. She didn't think the dream was worth mentioning; she could barely remember it.

When they finally landed in the airport in Sofia, Grace felt relieved. They had had to change flights a few times to get here, and she was over flying. They got off the plane and went and collected their luggage. They had to narrow down their life to a large suitcase each before leaving San Francisco. Rose nearly had a meltdown choosing which clothes to bring, but for Grace it was easy—jeans and tops, nothing fancy. They gave away most of their belongings to charities but stored what they wanted to keep in a shipping container. That way if they decided to stay somewhere for an extended period of time, they could get the container shipped over to where they were.

Once they had collected their luggage, Rose and Grace went to the pickup point that Rose had organized with her contact. They were to meet her just inside the main doors of the airport. When they got there, they spotted her straight away. A young lady with short red hair wearing a colourful dress walked up to them and greeted them. *What is with witches and colours?* thought Grace, amused.

"Hi, I am Rhea. Welcome to Bulgaria! I hope you had a good journey," said the young lady in English.

Grace held out her hand for her to shake, but Rhea grabbed her and pulled her into a tight embrace.

"Handshakes are for men; hugs are for sisters," Rhea said, squeezing Grace tightly.

Slightly shocked, Grace returned the hug and felt a warmth spread through her that made her relax.

"Hi, Rhea. I am Grace, and this is Rose. It's great to finally meet you," said Grace when they ended their embrace.

Rose stepped up to Rhea and also hugged her. "Oh, you are a pathokinetic!" exclaimed Rose as soon as they touched.

Rhea smiled. "I sure am! I knew you would be able to tell."

Grace looked at the two women confusedly. *A what now?* she thought.

As if Rhea had read her mind, she answered, "I have the ability to control emotion. What you just felt is how I greet people—my little gift to them."

Grace liked her immediately and knew they had made the right decision to help her.

"You speak very good English," said Grace.

"Thank you. I speak many languages. I aim to have friends from all over the world, so I need to be able to communicate with them," Rhea replied.

Grace felt as if she had wasted a lot of years not learning new things. She had thought she would be rid of this curse by now and hadn't bothered learning any new languages. Boy, did she regret this now.

"Come; let's go home so you can relax. You have to tell me all about the trip," Rhea said with a big smile.

Rhea had already got them a luggage trolley, and she helped them take their luggage to her car. When they got to the car, Grace chose to sit in the back seat so the witches could talk shop. This also allowed her to take in the scenery without getting distracted by conversation. Sofia was beautiful, and Grace especially liked the old-style buildings. She hoped she would find time to do the tourist thing while they were here. She could imagine herself walking around the streets and admiring the scenery for days.

It took about half an hour for them to get to their destination. Rhea pulled the car into the driveway of a quaint little cottage. The garden was filled with various herbs and beautiful flowers. The whole setup looked quite charming, and Grace secretly hoped they would spend a lot of time here. It was definitely a change from their city life in San Francisco. It would probably take her a few days to get used to the quiet again. Grace exited the car and went to the boot of the car to get her luggage.

"Your belongings are already inside," Rhea said with a wink.

Grace looked at the boot in surprise. "Oh, okay." She followed Rhea inside and saw her bags sitting in the entrance.

"Haven't you seen that done before?" asked Rhea. She must have seen Grace's bewildered expression.

"I don't usually use magic in front of Grace," said Rose.

Rhea looked at Grace, her face turned to sorrow. "I can see why you have trouble trusting magic, but magic can be good too. You'll see."

That surprisingly relaxed Grace's thoughts on magic a little bit. Even though she had just met Rhea, she knew she could trust her. Grace knew that Rose held back in the magic department a bit to respect her wariness towards magic. Perhaps it was time she loosen up a bit and let Rose live up to her potential.

The trio walked inside, and Grace and Rose sat on a long grey sofa in front of a big TV while Rhea went and got them refreshments. She returned later with a teapot and some cups and poured them all some tea. Grace blew on the hot liquid and took a tentative sip. *Mmm, heaven*, thought Grace.

"So, this werewolf?" said Grace. She had been burning with curiosity since Rose convinced her they were real.

"Oh yes," said Rhea. "Our little problem. About a year ago, there started to be reports of wild animal attacks in the area. I didn't think much of it until I noticed a pattern. They were all happening during the phase of the full moon: one night before the full moon, the night of the full moon, and then the night afterward. Shortly after, there was also some talk of a beast being sighted by some witnesses near where one of the attacks had happened—a big, hairy beast. So I did some digging. All my research pointed towards a werewolf, so I mixed up a potion that reacts to the magical properties in werewolf saliva. Then I had the hard task of finding an animal that had been attacked. It took two months, but eventually I found a half-eaten stag that the potion reacted to. That's when I decided to track down Rose. I heard that she was a powerful witch that was in need of help, so I thought we could help each other."

"Wow. What can we do to help?" asked Grace. She felt as if she were way out of her depth, but she wanted to help anyway.

"We have two more weeks until the next full moon, so until then we can research and plan, if that's okay with you guys. I need help with this. I am not the only one that has noticed the pattern of attacks, and it is starting to attract the wrong crowds. While I was looking for evidence I stumbled across a TV crew with night vision cameras and silver weapons. They looked ridiculous, but they could end up being dangerous. This werewolf is still a person, and the person may not even realize what is happening. I would hate for him or her to get caught and then they wake up in a cage where he or she would be experimented on. It could also expose the supernatural community, but that is easily dealt with. We have a contact in the media that can help with that."

Grace thought of what it would be like to wake up in a cage. That was another reason why she stayed under the radar. She once donated blood and received a phone call shortly after from someone at the labs who had tested it. This person was very excited and said that she hadn't seen anything like it before and asked if Grace would like to come in to do some tests so they could learn more about it. Grace almost agreed to until Rose pointed out that although her blood work was amazing, once they figured out how special she really was, she could get turned into a lab rat. Think about it, how useful would an immortal be to a government?

"We can start first thing in the morning," suggested Rose. "We can research lore, investigate the attacks, and then spread the word to see if anyone in the magical community has heard of any other werewolves. If we find people who have, we can they try to contact them and see if they can help us of give us some tips."

"That is a great idea! I knew I made the right decision

when I turned to you," said Rhea. "Also, while we are doing that, I'll make some enquiries about this coven you seek. I know they are in hiding, but I think once they get word of who you are and what you want to do, they should reveal themselves to you."

"Thank you for helping us," said Grace. It was good to have more people on their side.

"Not a problem. Go and get some rest. You guys look tired," said Rhea.

Grace felt tired too. The trip had been a long one, and all this talk of the supernatural had made her brain go into overdrive.

Grace was shown to her room. It had a big four-poster bed with magenta and purple bedding. It had so many pillows and cushions that Grace imagined lying on them would be like lying on a cloud. Rhea also showed Grace the en suite adjoining her room. It had a big bath with a shower on top. Grace looked at it with longing. It had been a while since she had a good soak in a tub. She ran the water and found some bubble bath in the cupboards under the sink. After the bath was run, Grace immersed herself into the water and felt herself relax. *Bliss. Absolute bliss.*

While in the tub, Grace thought about Solomon and what she was going to do when she found him. Truth be told, she wasn't sure what she could do. She had no powers, she couldn't fight to save her life, and she had nothing to intimidate him with. She just hoped that this coven Rose spoke of would have a solution for her.

Grace is walking down the same pebbled path
she walked before. She can't see much, as she

is again surrounded in a thick fog. Feeling frustrated, Grace starts to run along the path. Grace knows where she has to be. She comes upon the gates to the graveyard and stops to catch her breath. She watches as the fog recedes revealing the graves. Straightening up, Grace hears a distant voice call her name. She feels a longing for the voice. It feels like the thing she has been missing all her life. She knows that if she gets to the source of that voice, everything will be okay. Grace travels in the direction the voice is coming from, although she knows its source: the old headstone. She weaves through the graves, being careful not to step on any. Grace spots the headstone she is looking for and feels her heart skip a beat. She is ecstatic that she found it again. Running as fast as she can, she makes her way to the headstone. She is only a few rows away when her foot gets caught on a rock and she falls.

Grace woke up with a jerk. It was mid-morning, and she was grateful for having been able to sleep in. Her dreams had been plagued with cemeteries again, but she didn't dwell on it too long. She got dressed and went downstairs to find Rhea and Rose deep in conversation.

"… or we could try a locating spell. We just need to find some of its DNA. I think I have heard of a spell that could work. I just need to find it," said Rose

"That could work. Ah, good morning, Grace! I hope

you had a good sleep. We decided to let you sleep in a bit. Looked like you needed it," said Rhea, looking up.

"Good morning. I had a great sleep. That bed and the bath are amazing! Are you guys working already?"

"Yeah. I was up all night thinking of ideas," said Rose. "You know me; once I'm on to something, I won't stop."

Grace once watched Rose studiously work out a riddle that was written in a local newspaper. The answer was obvious to Grace, but Rose had tried to think outside the box, which led to a lot of frustration and a day of taunting from Grace.

"I am just going to have some breakfast; then I'll join in," said Grace. She hadn't eaten since the flight.

"Help yourself, darling," said Rhea.

"Thanks," replied Grace, and she went into the kitchen.

Grace looked through the fridge and pantry. This was the best-stocked kitchen she had ever seen in a house. She decided to make a stack of pancakes in case the other ladies where hungry too. Grace found cooking therapeutic, in that it gave her time to think. She thought about this werewolf and how the hell they were going to break it to the person about what had happened to him or her. Grace remembered back to her own realization of her situation. For a few months, she had walked around as if in shock. She kept seeing young couples with children and elderly couples walking along holding hands. Both were lives she would never know.

When the pancakes finished cooking, Grace loaded up a plate, grabbed some honey, and headed to the lounge.

"I hope you are hungry," said Grace as she put down the pancakes on the coffee table.

The two witches looked up at Grace then at the pancakes. Rose dug straight in—she had known Grace too long to show any manners—whereas Rhea went and got some plates.

"Thank you, Grace," said Rhea. "I was starting to get hungry. I didn't even have breakfast this morning. I was too engrossed in research."

Rose simply nodded and gave Grace a thumbs up. Grace nodded, knowing that Rose was also appreciative.

When the trio had finished their breakfast, Rose took the plates back to the kitchen and began to wash up.

"Rose is trying to find a locating spell. She thinks that if she can get some of the werewolf's DNA, she will be able to use the spell to locate him. It will even work when they are in human form," said Rhea.

"That would make looking for them easier," replied Grace.

"Yeah, but finding the right spell is proving to be difficult. The text Rose is looking at now is written in an old language that is nearly dead, so she is translating at the same time. She is truly remarkable," Rhea said, seemingly in awe.

Grace looked over at her long-time friend. Her brow was furrowed in concentration, and she had a pen in her mouth. She was seeing a whole new side to Rose. Usually when Rose concentrated on her magic, she was in her room, so Grace rarely got to experience it.

"What can I do to help?" asked Grace, keen to be part of the team.

"You could look at the newspaper reports to see if these animal attacks have any other patterns apart from happening during a full moon. If we can narrow down a location, it will make looking for them so much easier in case we can't get DNA for Rose's spell," replied Rhea.

"I can't read Bulgarian," said Grace, disappointed that she hadn't put her immortality to better use.

Rhea thought for a minute and then got up and left the room. Grace's eyes followed her out. A few minutes later, she returned holding a pair of glasses. She sat herself on the floor with her eyes closed and her legs crossed, holding the glasses with both hands. Rhea then started to chant in a language Grace had never heard before, and the glasses started to glow. Grace felt her heart rate quicken, and a panic rose in her chest. Rose stopped what she was doing, reached over and grabbed her arm, and gave it a reassuring squeeze. Grace grabbed her hand and held it until Rhea stopped chanting. Grace felt herself let out a breath that she hadn't even realized she was holding. Rhea then opened her eyes and smiled.

"Here, try these on," Rhea said while holding out the glasses.

Grace looked at them hesitantly and slowly reached out her hand.

"They are safe," said Rose. "If I'm not mistaken, Rhea has charmed them so that when you wear them you can read any language."

Grace grabbed the glasses and studied them. *They don't look sinister*, she thought.

"Can you use these to help you with the locating spell?" asked Grace.

"No. That language is a magic language, and charmed objects will not work on it. You have to earn the right to use that spell, and that means figuring it out without any magical aid," said Rhea.

That's fair enough, thought Grace.

"With these I can go to the library and see if they have a newspaper archive I can use," said Grace.

Sure, she could have used Rhea's internet, but she needed a bit of distance from magic talk after what she had just seen. Grace knew she had to get used to it eventually, but she felt a bit overwhelmed and needed to get out of the house.

"Sure. You can borrow my car. It has a GPS in it," said Rhea.

"Thank you. I'll head there now and see what I can find. I should be back for lunch."

"Okay," said Rhea, "we shall be here. If we come across anything of importance, we shall call you."

"Bye, Grace!" Rose yelled up from her book.

Grace enjoyed the drive to the library. She took a long route so she could see more of the city, and it was truly amazing. If things were different, she could have seen herself settling here for a while. Grace pulled up to the library and went inside. She walked through the front door and took a deep breath. *Nothing like the smell of books to get your blood pumping.* Grace put on her charmed glasses and walked around the large room, looking for signs of the archives. It was amazing to see the words of other languages turn into English. She found her way to a room at the rear of the library that had a sign reading "Archives" above it. Grace went in, made herself comfortable, and began her research. The newspapers were archived in filing cabinets, which Grace liked. She preferred the feel of paper to the look of screens. She opened up the most recent drawer and took out a month's worth of newspapers. "Beloved Dog Killed!" and "Animals on the Rampage!" were a couple of the headlines. She kept searching and noticed that the stories went back months. Grace could see that they were starting to attract attention. It was nearly lunchtime, and Grace had figured out that the attacks were taking place around the northern part of the city. *That narrows it down a bit,* Grace supposed to herself.

Grace looked at her watch. *Noon.* She supposed she had better head back to Rhea's house to see how the other two were progressing.

CHAPTER 4

It was the night before the full moon, and the trio were getting ready for their first night of hunting. Rose had fully translated the tracking spell and had gathered most of the items she needed. All she required now was some werewolf DNA, and they were hoping to find some tonight. While Rose was translating her spell, Grace was busy familiarizing herself with her newly acquired tranquillizer gun. Since she didn't have any magical abilities to help defend herself against the werewolf, this was the next best thing. One afternoon some time back, Rhea left the house to go do some shopping. When she returned, she had a big package with her. Grace was surprised when she was handed the package, and even more so when she opened it up to find the gun. Grace enquired where Rhea got it from, but Rhea just winked and said, "The less you know, the better."

Grace had never handled any sort of gun before, so she needed to practise. At first she used empty darts to practise shooting with in Rhea's backyard, but during the last few days she had gone out of town and practised over a distance. She wasn't a bad shot. She felt that as long as the werewolf didn't zigzag too much, she should be able to hit it. Grace smiled as she put her gear into Rhea's car. A month ago, she couldn't picture herself all dressed in black and wielding a weapon that could put a large animal to sleep, yet here she was. Trying to figure out the right dosage for the tranquillizer was tricky. They were not sure if it should be set to a smaller dose because of the werewolf's human side, or a lager dose because of its magical properties. They ended up consulting with a shape-shifting vet in Spain. He suggested the higher dose, as the werewolf's metabolism would be high so it could digest most of the night's catch before it reverted back to human form.

Once Rhea's car was loaded up with all their gear, they headed to their first destination. Rhea had mapped out a few areas that they were going to search first. They decided they would stick to the wooded areas. It may look suspicious if they were seen walking through the streets with a tranquillizer gun, dressed in black, and looking in people's backyards. When they got to their first location, they congregated around the bonnet of Rhea's car, where she laid out a map with a number of circled areas on it.

"I think we should search the same areas together. We are all new to this and don't know what to expect," said Rhea.

Grace and Rose both nodded in agreement. They let Rhea call the shots, as she knew the area better.

Rhea pointed to a spot on the map. "This is where I found the half-eaten stag. I think we should try this are first, as the werewolf has definitely been there at some point. If we find nothing there, we can try this area." Rhea moved her finger to another circle. "This is where a 'wolf-like' creature was spotted. If we still have no luck, I know of a watering hole nearby that animals frequent. Be careful, as there may be supernatural fanatics out trying to get their fifteen minutes of fame."

With the plan laid out, the ladies checked their packs. They all brought along some water, snack foods, and spare batteries for their torches. Even though the moon was bright tonight, the trees blocked out most of its light, making visibility poor. Grace double-checked her phone to make sure it had enough charge and a good signal. They decided to bring their phones along, but they had to keep them on vibrate. It is no good trying to sneak up on a werewolf when your phone is blasting its ringtone.

With Rhea leading the way, the girls set out to their first destination. Grace's nerves were on edge. She prayed that they would find the werewolf just sleeping under a tree, but she doubted she would be that lucky. Grace looked over at the two witches. Rhea looked like someone going for a casual stroll, and Rose looked as if she were observing the trees as though they were art. Rose's eyes met Grace's, and she gave her a reassuring smile. Grace returned it; her face must have given her away.

After walking for what felt like forever, Rhea came to a stop. "This is the spot," she announced.

Grace looked around. *I can't see anything too menacing … yet!* she thought to herself.

"I think we should split up," Rhea said. "That way we can cover more ground. If we each walk ten minutes in one direction and then turn around, we should cover a good area."

Grace really didn't want to be alone so soon, but she

didn't want to seem too afraid. So she just ignored her fears and boldly nodded.

"If anyone sees anything, call. Grace, if you see anything big and hairy, just shoot it. We will worry about what it is afterward."

Grace nodded. Her mouth was unusually dry, so she didn't even try to talk. Summoning all her courage, Grace chose a direction and started to walk, clutching her trank gun in front of her. She could hear the other two heading in different directions and hoped that they wouldn't go too far.

"Come on, Grace; you can't die! What are you afraid of?" Grace said to herself, hoping the self-given pep talk would make her brave. *Pain! I don't like pain!* Grace's subconscious yelled at her. Despite her internal struggle, Grace trudged on. She was determined to be a team player.

After ten minutes of tripping over sticks and jumping at shadows, Grace had found nothing. She turned around to head back to the rendezvous point. Along the way, she decided to walk a few metres off her original path so she wasn't going over the same ground again. Grace's eyes were scanning the woodland floor when she came across a huge paw print. She crouched down to get a better look. It had to be at least twenty centimetres long! Grace could feel her heart racing. She took a few deep breaths to clear her mind and hopefully settle her heart. The sight of the paw print made her realize how real all this was now. Grace struggled to figure out what to do next. Her mind was racing, and she needed to just stop and think for a second.

"Photo—I need a photo," Grace mumbled, pleased she had managed to think of something. She fumbled around with her pockets until her hands worked enough to get her phone out. Grace felt the hairs on her neck stand up on end, which made her look around. Satisfied nothing sinister was there, Grace quickly took several photos of the paw print. She thought for a moment and took one with her hand next to it so she could compare the size. Grace looked at her watch and decided it was time to head back to the others. She had spent quite a bit of time here, and she feared the others might be getting worried.

Grace found Rhea and Rose at the rendezvous point. They were deep in conversation and did not notice Grace as she approached them.

"Find anything?" Grace asked. They both stopped talking and looked at Grace with relieved looks on their faces.

"There you are!" Rose exclaimed. "We were just about to call you to see if you needed help."

"Sorry. I found a paw print and stopped to take some photos." Grace pulled out her phone and brought up the photos. She then passed it to Rhea, who flipped through the photos with Rose.

"Wow! That is big!" Rhea exclaimed.

"It looks recent too!" Rose added enthusiastically.

Grace felt her stomach drop. *Recent—as in not long before I came across it.* She wasn't sure what she would have done if she had seen the wolf. *Probably run screaming,* her subconscious chimed in. There was one problem with that scenario; Grace wasn't much of a runner. She'd never had to be one until now. *Maybe it's time I start to work out,* thought Grace. *Who knows what we are going to come across now that we have started to track Solomon more seriously.*

"Do you think you will be able to find the spot again?" Rhea asked, gesturing to the photos.

"I should be able to," replied Grace trying to keep her voice steady. Rhea passed Grace her phone back. Determined to hide her fear, she led them back to where she had found the paw print.

When they got there, Rose's eyed widened when she saw the print. "It's even more impressive in person!"

"Impressive" wasn't the word Grace would have use to describe it. "Horrifying" would have been close.

"I am pretty sure this print was made by our wolf. We should spread out from here and concentrate on this area tonight," said Rhea. She seemed alive with energy at the discovery.

Grace wasn't too thrilled about being separated again—especially since their werewolf must be close. They searched the area all night and did not find anything—no hairs and no more prints. Dejected, the weary trio headed back to the car and went back to Rhea's cottage so they could get some sleep. As soon as they walked through the door, Grace mumbled something along the lines of "good night" and headed to her room so she could shower and get some sleep.

> *Grace is walking along the same stone path, heading towards the cemetery. She is certain of her destination—the old gravestone. If only she could see what was written on it. Grace enters the graveyard though the gates and stops. "Grace," she hears. Knowing where the voice is coming from, she heads straight for the back of the cemetery, where the oldest*

graves are. The voice comes again, this time more urgent. "Grace!" Grace starts to run, and relief spreads through her when she sees the headstone. "I'm coming," says Grace as she starts to weave through the other graves. "Grace!" the voice says again, almost shouting. She van hear the voice echo around her. Grace approaches the grave she has been seeking and crouches in front of it, eager to see what is written on it.

Beep, beep, beep! Grace's alarm sounded loudly, waking her from her dream. She reached out her hand groped around until she silenced her alarm. Grace slowly sat up and noticed that she was covered in sweat and her heart was racing as if she had been running. She peered through her tired eyelids and checked the time. *Crap! An hour until sunset! I had better get moving.*

Grace got out of her four-poster bed and went into the bathroom for a quick shower. When she got out, she went over to the bathroom mirror and wiped the fog off so she could see her reflection. What Grace saw made her scream and turn around quickly. She had seen a huge dark shape standing right behind her, but now there was nothing there—just a blank wall. Turning back to face the mirror, Grace braced herself to see the shape again, but this time there was nothing—just her own reflection staring back at her, looking frightened. *Must have imagined it!* Grace cursed to herself. She then dried herself off and left the bathroom to get dressed, the whole time avoiding looking directly into any mirror.

Once Grace was dressed, she headed to the kitchen to get something to eat before they headed out again.

While Grace was eating, Rose came into the kitchen and sat with her. "You okay, Grace? I thought I heard a noise in your room."

"Yeah, I am good. I thought I saw something in the mirror, but I must have imagined it. I had not long woken up, so my mind was probably still in my dream," replied Grace.

"Was the dream of any interest?" asked Rose, watching Grace intently.

"Nah. I can't even remember it," lied Grace. She actually could remember it this time, but she didn't feel like sharing it with Rose.

An hour later, they were back on the road, with Grace riding shotgun. They decided to head back to the spot with the paw print, hoping that was one of the spots the werewolf frequented.

"Now tonight is the actual full moon," Rhea said while driving, "and legend has it that the werewolf will be at its fiercest and strongest, so be extra careful! During the day, I went to a butcher and got some cuts of meat. We'll see if we can draw it out with the scent."

Grace realized that Rhea was taking a different route than last night, and she had a feeling she knew where they were. Grace looked out of the car window and noticed that they were driving past a familiar-looking cemetery. She turned in her seat and watched it until it went out of her sight. It was only then that she noticed she had turned right around in the front seat and Rose was looking right at her from her seat in the back.

"Are you all right?" Rose asked her with concern on her face.

"Yeah, just thought I saw something," said Grace, and she turned back around in her seat. Rhea was also looking at Grace with a puzzled look on her face. Grace just stared straight out in front and hoped that they didn't ask any questions. She wouldn't know what to tell them if they asked. Grace was pretty sure that dreaming of the same cemetery wasn't a good thing in their world.

They arrived back at the woods and exited the car. Grace got her trank gun from the car boot and checked to make sure it was in working order, while Rhea grabbed some raw meat from a cooler. With all of them ready, they headed back to the spot where Grace had found the paw print the night before. Rhea and Rose were talking strategy while Grace's mind was stuck on that cemetery. She had no idea why, but she had the feeling she had to get to that cemetery, and soon.

When they reached the spot, Rhea and Rose started arranged the meat on the ground while Grace stood watch with the trank gun. When they finished, Rhea and Rose both had bloody hands from the meat. "Grace, could you please be a dear and reach into the bag on my back and grab out the water bottle. I can't do it with my hands so dirty."

"Sure," replied Grace, and Rhea turned around to give Grace better access to her backpack. Grace was rifling through the bag when something caught her eye. Looking more closely, Grace noticed it was Rhea's car keys.

"Grace."

The voice came from out of nowhere and startled Grace. She looked at Rhea and Rose, but they made no indication that they had heard it too.

"Grace," the voice said again. An image of the headstone from her dream popped into Grace's head, and she knew what she had to do. Grace grabbed the water bottle and handed it to Rose. Then, before she zipped the bag back up again, she grabbed Rhea's car keys, being careful to be quiet. While the two witches were busy washing their hands, Grace slowly started to back away from them as quietly as she could. When she thought she was far enough away, she quickly turned and ran towards the car, not caring how much noise she made. From behind her, she heard Rose yell out after her, but Grace just ran faster. She needed to get some distance on them.

Grace got to Rhea's car and threw the bag and tranquillizer gun on the back seat and turned the engine over. She put the car into reverse and slammed her foot down. The car headlights passed over Rose and Rhea, who must have chased after her. Both of their faces displayed identical looks of alarm. Grace didn't care; she just needed to get to that cemetery and find that headstone.

Even though Grace didn't know the way, she made it to the cemetery in no time at all. She pulled up at the cemetery gate and got out of the car. She didn't even worry about parking the car properly, which was so unlike her.

"Come to me, Grace," said the voice, radiating across the graves. Deep down, Grace knew that this wasn't right and that she shouldn't go, but she disregarded that feeling and ran across the cemetery. She knew exactly where to go, and nothing was going to stop her. Grace spotted the headstone she was seeking and headed straight for it. Her skin tingled as she drew closer. Grace finally reached the headstone and fell to her knees in front of it. The writing on it was strange and looked to be in another language, and Grace couldn't read it. She didn't have her enchanted glasses on her either. It looked like some sort of warning, but Grace ignored it and clawed at the earth in front of it. The ground was rock hard, and Grace's fingers started to hurt from raking at it. Frustrated at her lack of progress, she sat back on her heels and looked around. She needed something to help her. She got up off the ground and ran to the other side of the cemetery. There she found what she was looking for—the groundskeeper's shed. Grace walked up to it and tried the door. It was locked. *Damn*, she thought to herself. Not feeling put off, Grace walked around the shed and found a window that looked wide enough for her to squeeze through. The only problem was that it didn't look as if it could open. Looking around on the ground, she found a reasonable-sized rock and picked it up, testing its weight in her hand. She went back over to the window and hurled the rock through it, smashing a great big hole in it. Grace quickly looked around to check whether anyone was around, and then she pushed as much broken glass into the shed as she could, cutting her hands as she went. Once the window had most of the glass removed, Grace climbed up and crawled through the window, cutting her stealthy black clothes as she went. Grace fell inside the shed in a heap on the ground. Not wanting to waste time, she looked around and found what she was looking for—a shovel. She grabbed the shovel and exited the shed in the same way she had entered. Covered in cuts, scraps and dirt, she ran back to the grave and started to dig. She had no idea where she got the strength or stamina from, but she had to keep going.

Grace had no idea how long she had been digging when the shovel finally hit wood. She was covered in sweat, her hands were calloused, and she was sore all over. Grace got on her knees and used her hands to clear away enough dirt so she could see an inscription on the coffin. It was the same sort of writing as that on the headstone, and it seemed to display same sort of warning. Grace couldn't care less about what it had to say, and she raised the shovel above her head and brought it down as hard as she could and splintered the wood. She did this several times until she was able to use her hands to clear the wood away so she could see inside. At this point, the full moon was bright and high in the sky, so she could see quite well what was in that coffin. Peering into it, Grace saw an old, sticky corpse. It looked as if the body was still decomposing, which was strange, because judging by the age of the grave, there should have just been bones and rags. Grace noticed a metal rod sticking out between the corpse's ribs. Reaching down into the coffin, she clutched on to the rod and gave it an almighty pull. With a sickening squelching sound, the rod came free from the chest, and Grace fell back onto her heels.

Breathing heavily, Grace looked at the rod in her hand and then down at the body in the coffin. She felt sick to her stomach. What had come over her? Horrified, she threw the rod away as if it were poison. A sound brought her attention back to the corpse lying inside the coffin. It seemed as if it were vibrating. Grace knew she had to get out now. She was just starting to get up when the corpse's eyes shot open, and the piercing crystal-blue orbs locked on to hers. The corpse's mouth then opened, and two great big fangs elongated from the front of its mouth. Terrified, Grace stood up and clambered out of the grave as quickly as her shaking limbs would let her. She heard a sound come up from behind her, and she started to move more urgently. Once she was out and clear of the hole, she stood up, ready to run, but something grabbed her from behind and swung her onto the ground. She hit the earth hard, and it briefly stunned her. Grace turned over onto her back and tried to get up, but something pushed her back down. She looked along her arms and noticed some rotting hands were gripping her upper arms. Grace's eyes followed the rotting hands all the way up the rotting arms and all the way up to the rotting skull. It was the scariest thing Grace had ever seen. It looked as if it had no skin and had been dead for a long time. All its tendons and muscles were on display. Grace struggled and tried to wriggle out from under it, but the corpse was surprisingly strong. The corpse then increased its grip on her and bared its fangs. With one quick lunge, it brought its head down and latched onto her throat. Grace screamed as she felt its teeth pierce her flesh. She then felt it take mighty draws on her neck, moaning.

It's drinking my blood!

Grace started to panic and tried to push it off, but she could feel her strength ebb away with each draw the corpse took. After what felt like only a few seconds, Grace could feel her consciousness starting to slip away. The corpse on top of her was starting to feel heavier, and she had lost the strength to keep fighting it. Grace lay still now, staring across the graveyard, her vision starting to darken. The last thing she thought of before her world went black was that she had never been drained of all her blood before and that the recovery should be interesting.

CHAPTER 5

1574—York, England

It had been ten years since Grace and Leonardo got married, and Grace often reminisced about the early days. The wedding ceremony had been beautiful; and the feast afterward, enormous. Grace's father had spared no expense, and people had talked about it for weeks afterward. Grace's gown was amazing, and everyone in attendance complimented it. Even though they had to look for a new fabric merchant, they managed to get her dream gown made just in time. After the ceremony and festivities came the consummation. It wasn't quite what Grace had expected. The night before the wedding, Grace's father instructed one of the maids to tell Grace about what happens on the wedding night and what would be expected of her. The poor blushing maid had the talk over in minutes and then scurried off to complete her chores. Grace suspected that was just an excuse to avoid the talk. She didn't blame her, though; Grace had blushed just as much. Grace had the impression that it would be a magical experience, not an awkward one. The maid had failed to mention to Grace how much it would hurt and the bleeding that would take place afterward. Grace was mortified when she woke up the next day to find blood on the sheets. She thought something was wrong with her. Leonardo found her crying in bed the next morning and enquired what was wrong. When she told him, he just laughed and said that that was normal. Grace was a bit worried that it would happen again, but thankfully her husband's nightly visits were a lot better after the first time. At first he eagerly visited Grace in her bedchamber nightly, full of love and romance, but now he hadn't been with her for a long time. During the first few months of marriage, they went on outings together, attended festivities, and were always together. It was all laughter and talk of children. Leonardo was keen to become a father, and Grace was determined to make that happen. But after a year of no pregnancy, they started to drift apart.

It got worse when Grace's father suddenly died two years later, leaving her young sister, Marion, all alone. Grace had insisted on her sister moving in with them, as she was still young and needed a guardian. Leonardo was reluctant at first, saying that she would just be another mouth to feed and another body to clothe, but Grace managed to convince him. She told him that if they chose a suitable husband for her, everyone could benefit from the marriage. He told her that she could live with them until she was wed, and not a moment longer. Ever since her father died, all Leonardo was interested in was the land they had inherited. He would often stay out late and leave early in the morning, claiming that he had much work to do as her father's estates were in such a mess. Grace had trouble believing that. Her father was meticulous in every way, but it wouldn't do for a wife not to believe her husband. With Leonardo gone all the time, Grace and her sister were alone. Grace tried to spend time with Marion. She thought that if she could teach her how to be a lady, she would find a good husband like Leonardo; but Marion hadn't been the same since their father had died. She preferred her own company, which broke Grace's heart. Marion was all she had left.

A few years later, Leonardo came home drunk one night and woke Grace up. Grace thought he might have come for a nightly visit, but she noticed something was off. He was slurring his words, his clothes were a mess, and he smelt of wine. He grabbed Grace by the shoulders and shook her roughly, saying, "Where are my children?" Grace tried to reply, but Leonardo silenced her with a look, backhanded her, and left. Grace, feeling like a failure, cried for days. Leonardo stated that he had no memory of the event and she must have dreamt it. It was then that Grace decided to seek help. She went to numerous doctors, midwives, and even an apothecary. She had been bled, drank numerous concoctions, and slept with herbs under her pillow, but nothing worked. Grace was heartbroken and lonely. All she wanted to do was give Leonardo a child and have things back to the way they had been. Leonardo wasn't even interested in talks of getting Marion married any more. Whenever he brought it up, he would say that he was too busy to talk about things that were of little interest to him.

One morning, Grace started to feel quite sickly. She didn't want to say anything to Leonardo, as it seemed that lately she upset him whenever she came to him with a problem. By nightfall, Grace was so sick she fainted while at the dinner table, falling off her seat. When she came to,

Leonardo was bent over her and had a worried look on his face. He promptly sent a maid to get the doctor quickly.

"I will see you well, my love," said Leonardo as he helped her to her bedchamber, as she was too weak to walk. Even though Grace felt horrible, she smiled, thinking maybe things would get better. The doctor attended Grace and had a grave look on his face. He motioned for Leonardo to follow him out into the hall. Grace couldn't hear much, but from the tone the doctor used, she knew it didn't sound good.

"It's not fair!" Leonardo howled loudly. "Why must God punish us like this!"

Grace's heart dropped, and a tear left her eye; she didn't want to die yet.

That night he held her hand, praying, "Please, God, please." It went on like that for days, and every morning, he would check on her. It was the closest Grace had felt to Leonardo in a long time, and she was truly grateful. Her sister even visited her a few times. Grace must have looked a sight! Every time Marion came to see her, she was as white as a ghost when she entered the room and didn't stay long.

After nearly four weeks of being sick, Grace was finally starting to feel better and decided to go out to get some sun. She was tired of being inside, and it had been a while since she had been able to smell her roses. While she was out there, Leonardo approached her, surprising Grace. He grabbed her hand and said, "Sorry things have been so tough, my dear. Seeing you sick scared me. Now that you are feeling better, I want to take you somewhere special. Go and get dressed in your finest clothes and jewels and meet me outside."

Grace smiled broadly. Finally they'd get to spend some

time together. She had been a bit lonely lately, and the tension in the household had been quite high.

About an hour later, Grace met Leonard outside in her best clothes and jewels. She had spent quite some time ensuring that they would please her husband.

"You look just as beautiful as the day I met you!" Leonardo said. He too looked so gallant in his fine clothes.

"Thank you, my dear husband," replied Grace, thankful that her beauty had held. The only complaint she had was the scar left on her cheek. Solomon's cut had left a faint line there, but she was able to cover it up with powders.

Leonardo extended his hand and helped her into the coach, and he then followed her in. He sat across from her and smiled. Grace returned the smile and eagerly asked, "Where are we going, my love?"

"It's a surprise, my Grace," replied Leonardo with a wink.

Grace started to feel excited; it had been a long time since they had gone anywhere together, so she was really looking forward to it. The last time they went out together, a heavily pregnant tavern girl tried to get into their coach, but Leonardo roughly pushed her out. The girl wailed, as the fall must have hurt her. Grace felt sorry for her and moved to get out to help her, but Leonardo grabbed on to her arm harshly and forced her to sit down again. "It's just some poor whore beggar—nothing for you to worry about," he said with a sneer.

Grace wanted to argue the point, but she could feel the pain in her arm and decided it was best to keep quiet. She had made some enquiries a few days later into the girl's welfare, but it seemed she had disappeared.

The road they took was a rough one. Grace could feel each bump the coach went over. After a while, the coach pulled to a stop. "Ahh," said Leonardo, smiling. "Here we are."

Leonardo stepped out first. Grace waited for him to turn around so he could help her out, but when he didn't, Grace assumed it was because he was getting the surprise ready.

"You can come out now," said Leonardo.

Bracing herself for the surprise, Grace exited the coach. When she got out, she looked around. There were trees everywhere, and Grace did not recognize where they were.

"Where are we, my beloved?" Asked Grace, looking around at the trees.

Grace turned to Leonardo and watched as the driver of the coach walked up to him. Leonardo whispered something to him, and the driver looked over at Grace with a wicked grin. Leonardo then returned to the coach and retrieved a sack from the luggage compartment.

"It's all there as agreed," said Leonardo, and he handed the sack to the coachman, who reached in greedily and pulled out some coins. She watched the man put one in his mouth and test to make sure it was real.

Confused, Grace took a step closer to Leonardo to see what was going on, but Leonardo looked at her with such hate that it stopped Grace from moving any further.

"What's wrong, my love?" asked Grace, feeling anxious.

"What's wrong?" replied Leonardo in a voice that she had never heard before. "You are what's wrong. We have been married for ten years now, and you still bear me no children!"

Grace felt a pain in her chest as her heart broke. She

had thought that they were past this and were starting to get close again.

"I've been trying," Grace said, feeling her eyes prickle with tears. "I've asked everyone for help, but nothing works."

"Well then obviously something is wrong with you. The reason you have been sick the last few weeks is because I have been poisoning you. It should have worked. I used half as much on your father, and he died like he was supposed to. Not you, though. You still curse me with your presence and barren body."

Grace couldn't hold the tears back any more. "You killed my father!" Grace exclaimed.

"Yes. Nature was taking too long, and he was just wasting his time with the land. I can do so much more with it," replied Leonardo.

Grace was sobbing uncontrollably now. It had turned out her sweet Leonardo was a monster.

"Why would you want to kill me?" she sobbed.

"I have no more use of you. Ever since I stopped coming to your bed, I have been attending to your sister in her bed. She managed to achieve what you didn't. She is with child, my child. The doctor has confirmed it. I need you dead so I can marry your sister. That way I still get heirs and still get to keep your lands."

Grace felt as if she was going to be sick. *My own sister.* They weren't overly close because of the age difference, but she couldn't believe that Marion would do this. *Solomon was right!* she thought with dismay.

"Enough talk. We have come here to remedy the situation." Leonardo turned to the driver and said, "Make it look real."

Grace watched as the man clenched his fist, drew his arm back, and then punched Leonardo in the face, knocking him to the ground. Grace screamed and took a few steps back, but she tripped on her dress and fell. Leonardo then got up and touched the blood coming from his lip.

"Perfect," he said. He then proceeded to rip and scuff up his fine clothing.

Grace watched in horror as the man she had loved rearranged his clothing to make it look as if he had been in a scuffle.

He then looked down at Grace and said, "Farewell, Grace." Then he started to walk off into the woods.

Grace watched him walk away in disbelief until a shadow came across her. Looking up, she saw the driver holding a large knife. Grace turned over and tried frantically to crawl away. The man stepped up to her and grabbed her bonnet. Grace pulled forward so the bonnet slipped off her head. The man threw the bonnet on the ground and grabbed Grace by her hair, snapping her head back. With his other hand, he brought the blade around the front of her and sliced it clean across her throat. Blood sprayed everywhere, and Grace's vision swam. The man put the knife on the ground and turned Grace over, shoving her hard onto the ground. Grace grasped at her neck to try to stop the bleeding while coughing and gurgling blood. The pain was unbelievable, but it was not as bad as the pain in her racing heart. The hired killer then started to roughly rip off the beautiful jewellery Grace had picked out especially for her outing. He then got up and walked out of her vision. Lying there feeling numb and in shock, Grace welcomed death. There was nothing left for her in this life. Her husband despised her, and her sister had betrayed her. She was truly alone. She closed her eyes and waited for her life to fade. She was broken and had nothing left.

After a few moments, Grace noticed she was breathing a bit better and wondered if this was it. She opened her eyes and looked around. No, she was still in the same place. Grace saw the man who had cut her standing by the coach. It looked as though he was counting the money in the sack that Leonardo had handed him. She also saw the discarded knife on the ground near her. The hurt turned to anger, and Grace forced herself to sit up. The pain in her throat was enough to make her pass out, but she struggled through it. She reached over to the knife and grabbed it. If she was going to die, she might as well take her killer with her. She rose to her feet and stood up with the knife held in front of her. She took a tentative step forward and then bent over and vomited blood all over the leafy floor. The sound of Grace expelling her stomach made the man jump and turn around. His eyes widened when he saw Grace upright, covered in blood, and a look of terror spread across his face. After Grace finished vomiting, she straightened and pointed the knife at the man and took a step forward.

"Y-y-you should be dead!" he stammered in a rough voice.

Grace opened her mouth to talk, but only a croak came out. She surmised he must have cut her deeply, which made her angrier, so she tried to scream.

An awful screech came out of Grace's mouth, and the man dropped everything in his hands. "Witch … witch!" was all he could say while backing away from her. Grace just nodded. *May as well let him think that. Let it add to his fear.* The man then turned away and sprinted into the woods.

Grace waited until she could no longer see the man and then sank to the ground where she sat and tried to make sense of what just happened. She looked at the knife in her hand that was covered in her own blood and threw it away in disgust. Overcome with emotions, Grace lay on the leaf-covered ground and thought of her life and how unfair it had been. She was meant to have married well, given birth to a throng of children, and lived happily ever after. Now look at her. After a while of just lying on the ground, staring at the trees above her, Grace noticed that the pain in her throat was starting to feel better. She carefully reached up to her neck to find that the wound had stopped bleeding. *Maybe this is purgatory,* Grace thought, and she gave the cut a quick poke. *Ouch! No—still alive.*

How on earth did I survive? thought Grace. She turned her head and looked over at the coach and noticed that the would-be killer had dropped all of the loot in his panic to get away. Seeing the abandoned valuables lying on the ground brought a small smile to her face. At least the thug was running scared and she got to keep his fee. She got up slowly, made her way over to the coach, and picked up the items; it seemed unfair to leave them in the dirt. She then climbed inside the coach so she could think without distractions. She couldn't go home, and she had no other family. She looked at the bag of loot in her hands again and did a quick calculation. *This could be enough to start over*, she thought. She needed to get far away. If she were to sell the horse and coach, she should have enough to bribe a captain to take her across the sea. There was nothing for her here any more, and if she stayed, Leonardo would try to kill her again.

Grace emerged from the coach and sat in the driver's seat. Picking up the reins, she was unsure of what to do. Thinking back to what she had seen her drivers do, she flicked the reins, and the horse started to move. Grace breathed out a sigh of relief and let the horse choose its own path. Grace had no idea which direction they were heading, but she hoped it would lead them to a town.

Grace navigated the coach through the thick trees as best she could. She didn't really need to, though, as the horse was quite apt at finding its own way. Since she had always had drivers to take her places, she had never needed to know how to drive a horse and coach. Wasn't this a learning curve for her! Grace just hoped that wherever they were headed, it was far away from York and even further away from Leonardo.

Grace used the solitude to reflect on the last few years. The more she thought about it, the more things started to fit together. Just before her father passed, Leonardo had spent a few evenings there. He told Grace that he was helping with her father because he had seemed sickly lately. When Grace expressed concern, Leonardo told her not to worry. How wrong he had been! When they had just got back from her father's funeral, Leonardo was already absorbed in the lands they had inherited. Grace's eyes started to prickle with tears, and her chest felt hollow. Her horrid husband had robbed her of her time with her father. They had been quite close. A tear ran down her cheek as she remembered how well he had provided for her and her sister.

A lump formed in Grace's throat when her thoughts

turned to Marion. She didn't want to hate her sister, as it wasn't in her nature, but she didn't feel like liking her at the moment. Grace would never do that to her. Sleeping with another woman's husband was unthinkable, let alone one's sister's husband. Even worse was that that affair had resulted in a pregnancy! Grace shook her head and then felt up to her throat. The cut the hired killer had made was all but healed. If it hadn't been for the blood that was spilt down Grace's fine gown, no one would have been able to tell what had happened. Grace prayed that the would-be killer was still running scared. It was the first time she had ever had to threaten someone, and she hoped it was the last. She was not a violent person and shuddered at the thought of it, but in the end her survival instincts had kicked in. That, and for some reason her mortal wound had healed miraculously quickly. An image of Solomon's face appeared in Grace's mind, and she remembered back to the night he attacked her and the strange events that followed. She also remembered her father's face when he informed her they had found items that belonged to a sorcerer. Solomon's voice seemed to radiate in her head when she remembered his last words to her: "I wish you a long and happy life then!"

It was late in the afternoon when Grace finally saw a town on the horizon. She let out a sigh of relief and relaxed a bit. *Finally, a town!* She had been starting to get worried she would never see one again. The next thing she had to worry about was her clothes. They were covered in dirt and blood, and she was sure people would flee when they saw her. She pulled on the reins, and the horse stopped, making Grace feel quite proud. She felt maybe she could make it on her own. She got down, went inside the coach, and took one of the curtains down to wrap around herself. *This will have to do*, thought Grace in her makeshift shawl. *Hopefully it will be dark soon and no one will notice.* She entered the town and looked around for an open dress shop. She wanted a simple dress so she wouldn't stand out. She found a suitable dress shop and went in. The store owner was sitting behind the counter with a small boy. The shopkeeper regarded Grace with raised eyebrows.

"We close soon," he said flatly. Grace showed him a coin, and his expression changed to one of interest. He stood up and greeted her. Grace pulled the coach curtain around her tighter and pointed out a dress that was hanging up. She wasn't sure if her voice was working yet, so she gave a little cough and said croakily, "I wish to buy that dress, along with a few others." Relief spread through her. Her voice was a welcome sound to her ears. "I also require a travelling bag that I can put the dresses in." There was no permanent damage, by the sound of it. The shopkeeper thought for a moment and then turned to the boy and said, "Lad, please run down to Arthur's shop and purchase a bag for this lady. Tell him I shall send you back with the money after."

The little boy's face lit up, and he ran from the shop. The poor darling must have been bored in the shop all day with no one to play with. Grace regarded him with sorrow. She could have had a child that age.

The shopkeeper grabbed the dress and collected a few more from a shelf and asked if she would like them wrapped.

"I wish to wear one of them now," replied Grace.

The shopkeeper directed her to a back room so she could change.

"May I please have a bowl of water to freshen up too?

I have travelled a long way," said Grace, holding up a coin. The man accepted it without hesitation and went and got her a bowl.

Grace went into the back room and changed. She couldn't stand the sight of her old dress and crumpled it on the ground. After Grace had finished cleaning herself up, she felt so much better. All the blood and dirt had been washed away, and she had fresh clothes on. She left the back room, and the boy had returned with a decent-sized travelling bag that the shopkeeper had already packed for her.

"Would you be so kind as to dispose of my old dress for me? I have no need for it," Grace asked the shopkeeper.

"Of course, ma'am," said the man, bowing. "May I be of any more assistance?"

Grace thought for a moment. "I wish to sell my horse and coach. Know anyone that will give me a fair price that will be open?" she enquired.

The store man thought for a bit and said, "Try the stables. If you keep following the road, turn right at the blacksmith's and keep going. You can't miss it, my lady."

"Thank you for everything," she replied.

Grace finalized the sale and turned to leave.

As she was heading to the door, the shopkeeper asked, "Do you require a bonnet?"

"No, I am not married," replied Grace, hoping that she'd hidden the sadness in her voice.

Grace got up on her coach and followed the shopkeeper's instructions, and soon enough she came across the stables. She got down and looked for someone to talk to. She found a stable boy and asked him to fetch his master. He ran off and came back with an overweight man who was huffing, puffing, and red in the face. He looked annoyed, as if he had been interrupted, but his demeanour changed when he saw what Grace had to offer. They negotiated for a bit, and he agreed to give Grace a small sum as well as a ride to the docks. Grace felt as though he may have cheated her in price, but she didn't mind. She just wanted to get out of here.

Once Grace got dropped at the docks, she looked at the big ships. She had never been this close to them before. Leonardo didn't think it was a woman's place to be near ships. She prayed that none of the captains shared the same view. She walked up to the dock master and asked him which boat was leaving first. He pointed her to a big one a few docks down. She pulled her luggage along and stopped by the ramp of the ship and waited for someone to walk past. A man carrying a case headed her way, and she tried to stop him, but he kept going. The next man was reading a piece of paper, and he ignored her also. Feeling annoyed, Grace stood in the way of the next sailor, who had his arms full of food.

He pulled up just before he ran into her. "Out of my way, lady!"

"Only if you get your captain for me," Grace stated boldly.

The man sighed and then yelled, "Hey, Captain!"

Grace turned and looked up the ramp, and a man appeared at the top of it. "Who is calling me?"

"This 'ere lady wants a word!" replied the man holding the food.

The captain walked down the ramp, and Grace moved out of the way so the captain could come down and the crew member could go about his errands.

"You wanted a word?" said the captain in a rough voice. He was tanned all over and looked as if he needed a good bath.

"I heard your ship is leaving soon. I can pay you well if you take me with you," said Grace.

"Why would you want to do that?" the captain sneered.

"There's nothing for me here. All my family has died, and I wish to start a new life elsewhere." Grace hoped she wouldn't give away the lie.

The captain grunted turned away. Grace reached out and grabbed his arm. He frowned at looked at her hand, but then his face changed when he saw the ruby ring that was still on Grace's finger.

"I can give you this plus more if you just let me on your ship. I promise I won't be a burden," Grace pleaded.

"Do you even know where we are going?" he asked.

"I don't care," replied Grace.

"Fine," said the captain. "You can have my cabin, but you stay in there. I won't have you distracting my men. The food won't be great either."

Grace shrugged. She didn't have much of an appetite at the moment anyway.

He picked up Grace's bag for her and went up the ramp. Grace followed him up, trying not to look down into the water below. He showed her to a room that had a strange smell about it and housed an untidy bed. He put Grace's bag down and then looked at her expectantly. Grace pulled the ring off her finger and gave it to him. She then reached into the bag and got out the necklace she had been wearing when Leonardo's hired hitman had tried to kill her, and she gave that to the captain as well, followed by a few coins. Pleased with what she had given him, he handed her a key and said, "Lock the door behind me, and keep it locked."

He then left the room and shut the door behind him. Grace went over to the door and locked it. She put the key in the lock and felt the door latch. *At least I will be safe*, she thought. She moved a chair over to the window and waited. When the ship finally set sail, Grace watched the land disappear from view with tears streaming down her face. She had to find a way find a way to end this. She had to find Solomon.

CHAPTER 6

Present day—location unknown

Grace's eyelids fluttered as she slowly regained consciousness. Her head was still a bit foggy, but she could make out the distinctive humming and beeping of machines surrounding her. She slowly opened her eyes and waited for them to adjust. The room was dimly lit, so it didn't take long. As far as she could tell, she was in some sort of hospital. She recognized some of the equipment connected to her from when she was studying nursing, but the room was a bit different to any hospital that she had done her work experience in. For one, there were bars on the windows. Grace tried to sit up to get a better look around but found that her left wrist was restricted. She gave her arm a jerk and heard a metal-on-metal jingle. She threw back the blankets so she could look at what was making the sound and saw that her wrist was shackled to the bed. *Crap, crap, crap!* Grace thought to herself. The door to her room opened, and a tall man walked in. He was of slim build with short, dark hair and grey eyes, and he was wearing a smart-looking suit.

His presence seemed to make the room feel cooler, and it made Grace shiver.

He started to speak in Bulgarian, but Grace, not understanding what he was saying, shook her head. He tried another language, this one sounding like German, but again Grace shook her head. "English," she said, hoping that he could understand her.

"Ah, yes, English. That would have been my next guess," said the man with a heavy accent. "It is so good to see you awake. I am Dr. Werner, and this is my research facility." He swept his arm in an arc to indicate the room they were in. Grace looked around at the room, starting to feel alarmed. *This cannot be good.*

"Why am I here?" asked Grace, even though she already knew the answer.

Dr. Werner walked to the end of her bed and looked at her. "Your body was found outside of a hospital in Bulgaria; it seems the vampire that drained you of your blood gave you the courtesy of dropping you off."

Grace looked at the doctor confusedly. "Vampire? What do you mean?"

"When you came into the hospital, there were distinctive puncture marks on your neck. Even though I didn't get to see it in person, the mortician that was on duty took pictures and made detailed notes of it."

Grace reached up to her neck but felt smooth skin. She realized that if the wounds were already healed, she must have been out for a few days. "How did I end up here?" she queried.

"Well, you suffered significant blood loss, and all revival attempts failed. The on-duty doctor pronounced you dead.

They took you down into the morgue, and the mortician started the autopsy. When he began his first incision across your chest, he noticed something strange—you were bleeding. For someone who was pronounced dead due to blood loss, you bled a lot. The poor mortician nearly had a heart attack and quickly called for a doctor to give him a second opinion. The doctor checked your signs and found a very faint heartbeat that wasn't there before. He should know; he was the one that pronounced you dead. That same doctor also owed me a few favours. Once he realized you had come back from the dead, he gave me a call."

"Why?" Grace asked.

"I am not a normal doctor. I seek answers to life's mysteries through unconventional methods. I also have a great deal of knowledge about what else the world has to offer. I know vampires are real; I have two. I also have a shape-shifter, a mind reader, and a girl whose powers are so extraordinary it makes my hair curl to think about it. I was in the area, hunting a werewolf to add to my collection, when I got the phone call regarding you."

Grace's heart was pounding in her chest. This doctor was clearly evil and needed to be stopped. She knew she had to find a way out of here and, if she could, rescue his other captives. Grace summoned all her courage and looked Dr. Werner straight in the eyes. "I'm not sure what you are talking about," Grace said defiantly.

"Oh come on, now; let's not play games. My scientists did a workup of your blood while you were sleeping, and its properties are amazing. You heal at an astonishing rate, and that is something that needs to be explored. I have already started doing some experiments of my own. You see, I am actually seventy-six years old. I had my lab give me a blood transfusion using your blood, and it turned back my biological clock. Only a week ago, I was riddled with arthritis and had to wear glasses to see; now look at me." He held out his arms and gestured to himself.

He certainly didn't look seventy-six years old at all. He looked to be in his early thirties at best. Grace looked at the machines again and noticed that one of them was hooked up to a vein in her arm. She watched it in revulsion as her blood travelled out of her arm and into a blood bag.

"It took a bit of adjusting, but we have managed to get the flow rate right. We are taking just enough blood to keep you awake. If you prove to be difficult, then we can increase the flow enough to keep you permanently unconscious. You are a curious creature, and I hope to gain much knowledge from you."

Grace tried to move her hands to her face, but she had forgotten about the handcuffs, which gave a loud jangle.

"Oh yes, the handcuffs. I cannot let one of my prize possessions escape, now can I?"

Grace stared at the doctor with disgust. *What a despicable human being!*

He walked over to Grace and brushed her cheek with the back of his hand. Grace jerked back and glared at him. She couldn't stand to be touched by him, knowing what kind of person he was.

"Come on, now. Don't look at me like that. I am going to provide you a nice home with others just like you, and you will provide me with the secrets to your special abilities." Dr. Werner chuckled and then left the room.

Grace rested her head back on her pillow and stared up at the roof above her bed. She was truly trapped.

The next day, Grace was woken up by a nurse who put on some gloves and told Grace she was going to remove her catheter. Grace wanted to refuse, but the nurse said she could always call someone to help hold her down. Not wanting an audience, Grace complied and stayed still while the nurse did her thing. About an hour later, a group of people entered her room and surrounded her bed. They were all carrying clipboards and looking at her with great interest. Grace felt uncomfortable and crossed her arms across her chest. She felt quite exposed wearing only a hospital gown.

Not long after the group entered, Dr. Werner strolled in. He gave Grace a big smile. "Good morning! All these people work for me, and they are going to help me unlock your secrets." That smile of his gave Grace a deeply unsettling feeling. Dr. Werner then addressed the group in a language Grace didn't recognize. They all nodded eagerly and looked Grace over. Dr. Werner gave a whistle, and a nurse entered the room along with two big men dressed in black. The nurse headed over to Grace and started to remove her tubes while one of the big men removed her handcuffs. Before Grace could rub her wrists, they grabbed her off the bed and put her into a wheelchair—none too gently, either. There they put the handcuffs on again. Grace looked at the chains in sadness. She hoped that her life wouldn't become a life of chains and people looking at her.

One of the big men dressed in black went around the back of the chair and began to push her towards the door. Dr. Werner hurried his pace so he was in front and led them out the door. When they left the room, Grace looked behind and noticed that all the people in the room had begun to follow them. Grace sat forward again and watched the back of Dr. Werner's head, imagining all sorts of things that a good girl shouldn't.

Dr. Werner ran many tests on Grace that left her exhausted, both physically and mentally. First it was a series of scans. That was the easy part. All she had to do was lie on a table. Then they made her walk on a treadmill with probes stuck to her. Her results must have been pretty average, as the group of people didn't look very impressed. Knowing that they were unimpressed with her walking made her give a little victory smile. What did impress the clipboard-holding group was when Dr. Werner stuck her in a tube lying down. Grace wasn't sure what it was for. She thought it was another machine that would scan her again. Looking around, Grace noted that it seemed airtight and only a few hoses connected to it. It wasn't until it started to fill with water that she began to panic. Realizing the intent behind the tube, Grace started to scream and bang on the glass surrounding her. She looked towards the group of people, hoping one of them would help her, but they just watched her with a professional interest. Grace knew she wouldn't die, but she didn't relish the idea of constantly drowning. She had experienced drowning once before, and it hadn't been pleasant.

When the water was almost at the top of the tube, Grace took one last gasp of air and waited. Once she was fully submerged, she realized how eerily silent it was under the water. She tried to look out of the tube, but her hair was flowing around her. Grace tried to relax and not panic, hoping to ride this out for as long as she could. After a while, her chest began to ache and spasm. With one cough, all the air that Grace had held was released, allowing water to be sucked in. She coughed some more when the water hit her lungs, making them scream in pain.

After about a minute of thrashing around, Grace just stopped. Her lungs had stopped fighting the water. It did hurt not to breathe, but Grace was exhausted and just floated in the water. It was oddly peaceful. It seemed like a lifetime before the water started to drain out of the tube. Grace watched the air bubble grow bigger, and she embraced it as it came towards her. When the water was gone, Grace gave a little cough and then expelled all the water that was in her lungs and stomach. Grace finally got the last bit of water out and managed to suck in some air. As welcoming as it was, it hurt to breathe. Grace was lying on her side when the tube opened, and the two men dressed in black lifted her out. They put her back in the wheelchair and handcuffed her again.

Whilst Grace was sitting in the wheelchair, a nurse came and made a series of observations. Grace glared at the men and women surrounding her as hard as she could, hoping they would notice. None of them did. They were all chatting excitedly about what they had just seen and were scribbling down notes with much enthusiasm. A towel was roughly thrown over Grace, and they wheeled her back to her room. The nurse helped Grace change her gown, and then she was secured to the bed again. Grace's chest hurt most of the night, making it difficult for her to sleep. After tossing and turning as much as she could, she finally fell into a deep sleep.

The next day, Grace was visited only by a nurse and a man who brought her food. Grace was relieved; she didn't feel much like having people look at her.

That night Grace was woken up by a tall man dressed in a doctor's coat walking through the door. She peered through an eyelid, expecting Dr. Werner, but was surprised when it wasn't him. This man was taller—at least six feet tall—and had black hair and a body built like an athlete's. Grace couldn't see his face, as he had his back turned to her, but when he turned around, Grace noticed his eyes straight away.

She could swear she had seen them before. As he looked around the room, Grace realized they were the same crystal-blue eyes that the corpse had. Grace stared at him with confusion. She parted her lips to talk, but he held his finger up to his mouth.

"Shh," the man said, walking over to Grace. "My name is Vitus, and I am going to help you." He had an old accent that she couldn't quite place.

All Grace could do was nod. This man looked like a God, and his voice was amazing. He could have been a narrator or a public speaker with a voice like that. She wasn't sure what he had said, but she would agree to pretty much anything that came out of that mouth. Vitus walked over to the side of the bed with the handcuffs and grabbed them. In one swift move, he snapped them open. The sound of the handcuffs breaking brought Grace's attention back to reality.

"It's you!" she exclaimed. "You were the body in that grave!" Grace realized that it was his voice that had lured her to the cemetery and to her frantic digging.

"Yes, I was, and I am so sorry!" Vitus said.

Grace attempted to talk again, but Vitus cut her off.

"I'll explain everything later," said the man, nervously looking over at the door.

"What did you do to me?" demanded Grace.

"I know you are upset, but please let us get out of here before anyone else comes into this room," pleaded Vitus.

Grace saw the sense in that and pushed back the covers and swung her legs over the side of the bed. She grabbed at the leads coming from her and ripped them out, not caring about doing any more damage. She stood up and moved towards the door, eager to get out of the room. It took a few steps for Grace to realize that she was dressed in only a hospital gown with the back undone. Grace quickly reached around the gown and gathered it so it covered her ass. Vitus didn't seem to notice. He walked up to the door and opened it and peered through a small opening.

"The way is clear," Vitus said, and he stepped out into the hallway.

Grace hesitated. After what happened in the grave yard, she wasn't sure she could trust him. Vitus sensed her hostility and stood facing her with his hand out to her. "You can trust me," he said in the most sincere voice.

Grace looked at him and thought, *Stuff it; what have I got to lose!* Throwing caution to the wind, Grace grabbed Vitus's hand and felt a frisson go up her arm. She had never felt anything like it before, but she liked it. Vitus gave her hand a quick squeeze and led her into the hallway. He started down a long hallway with doors all along it, with Grace in tow. His grip on Grace's hand was strong and comforting. They got to a *T* intersection in the hallway, and

Vitus pressed himself against the right wall. Grace followed suit. She had no idea what else to do; she had never been in a situation like this before.

Vitus turned to Grace and grabbed her face with both hands. "Stay here. I have an idea." He turned and went down the corridor.

Grace leaned against the wall and waited. While waiting, Grace used this opportunity to have a look around. She noticed that there were quite a few doors down this hall. She also noticed that there were some broken cameras hanging from the ceiling.

A minute later Grace heard a sound coming from the corridor that Vitus had gone down. She chanced a peek and saw him walking down the hallway, wheeling a wheelchair with a blanket on it. He pulled up the wheelchair next to Grace and said, "Get in."

Grace hesitated. "I can't," she said.

Vitus looked anxious. "Why not?" he asked hurriedly.

"There are others here that need help," Grace replied.

Vitus grabbed grace by the shoulders and looked her in the eye. "If we make it out of here tonight, I promise I will come back with you at a later time to free them. We don't have much time and need to go now!"

Grace thought for a second; she was in no shape to pull any heroic rescues tonight. She hopped into the wheelchair, threw the blanket over herself, and gripped the armrests as Vitus steered her down the corridor.

"I came through a door a few corridors over. If we can get to that door without being noticed, we stand a good chance of getting away," said Vitus.

Grace looked up at Vitus. His face was lined in deep concentration.

After they had gone down several corridors, they rounded a corner. "There. That's the door I came through," Vitus said with relief in his voice. He picked up the pace, pushing the wheelchair faster. Vitus stopped the wheelchair just in front of the exit and grabbed Grace's hand. He took one look in Grace's eyes and then pushed through the door.

On the other side, the sounds of guns cocking caught Grace's attention. Even though it was dark outside, she saw armed men crouching down with various guns in their hands. Right in the middle was Dr. Werner, wearing a smug look on his face. "Good try! I am not sure who you are, but you stealing something that belongs to me."

"I belong to no one!" shouted Grace defiantly. She couldn't believe the nerve of this man. She was determined that if she escaped this, she would personally ensure that his "special beings" would be freed and his research facility shut down.

Vitus turned to Grace and grabbed both her hands. "Do not be afraid." He lifted one up to his mouth and gave it a little kiss. Grace felt a pulse go through her hand. Vitus dropped her hands and faced the armed men. He changed his stance to a fighting one and let out a mighty roar which made his features look primal. Grace stepped backwards until her back hit the closed door behind her. Vitus crouched on his powerful legs crouched and then leapt from where he was standing and charged at the first man. The man fired at Vitus, but he managed to dodge the bullet in a blur. He streamed past the gunman and stood behind him. With one swift movement, he grabbed the man's head with both hands and gave it a quick twist. Grace heard the crack from where she stood, and her knees gave way and she felt bile build up in her throat.

Vitus then moved on to the next armed man and knocked him to the ground with one quick punch. Grace watched the mayhem in front of her. Her saviour had turned out to be some kind of animal. Grace's eyes found Dr. Werner, who was watching Vitus with great fascination. Grace turned back to the chaos and watched the blur that was Vitus take out the men one by one. When most of his men had fallen, Dr. Werner looked towards Grace and nodded. He then grabbed two of his men and walked away.

After the last armed man had fallen, Vitus stopped and stared at Grace. He was sweating and breathing hard, and he was covered in blood. Grace wanted to be repulsed by his actions, but instead she was absorbed in his grandeur. He took off the doctor's coat he had been wearing and used it to wipe his face and hands clean of blood, and he then discarded it on the ground among the broken bodies. Grace weaved her way through the bodies over to him and grabbed his hand. Even though he was some sort of killer, she felt safer with him.

Vitus must have noticed that Grace was struggling to keep her hospital gown closed, as he had taken off his shirt and handed it to her. He was wearing a singlet underneath, and it looked damp with sweat. Grateful, Grace pulled the shirt over the top of the gown; she didn't feel like getting undressed in the middle of nowhere in front of a man she had just met. They headed towards the giant wall that was surrounding the building they had just escaped. When they reached, it Vitus said, "Step into my hands, and I will lift you up. He put his back against the wall and made a foothold with his hand. Grace looked up at the wall and then at Vitus, who was looking at her expectantly. It was still a long way up, even if Vitus stretched. She walked up to Vitus and grabbed his shoulders and put her foot in his hands. This was the closest Grace had been to him since he had drained her blood, and he smelt good.

"On the count of three, I am going to throw you up. When you reach the top, try to get on to the ledge. I'll be right behind you," said Vitus.

"What?" Grace breathed. She was too enthralled by his voice to pay attention.

"One …" Vitus began.

"Hang on," Grace cut in.

"Two …"

"No, wait! What do I do?" A panicked Grace shouted, gripping Vitus's shoulders.

"Three!"

As soon as the word had left his mouth, Grace felt herself get thrown into the air as if she weighed nothing.

Grace saw the top of the wall coming in fast, so she desperately reached out with both hands and latched on to it. She managed to keep a grip on the wall and pull herself up enough so she could get it under her armpits. She tried to use her legs to push herself up more, but her bare feet had no grip, and she wasn't that agile. Grace felt a breeze go past her and saw a pair of rather large shoes appear next to her. A pair of large hands grabbed her under the armpits and hoisted her up onto the wall. Grace felt her feet touch the top of the wall, and one of the hands let go so she could find her balance. Grace looked down and saw how high she was. *Whoa!* She reached over to Vitus, who had helped her up, and grabbed onto his arm tightly.

"It's okay. I'll catch you." He took her hand off his arm and jumped down.

Grace looked down at him with an open mouth as he looked up. It was then that she remembered she wasn't wearing any underwear! Not worried about the fall any more, Grace frantically tucked the hospital gown between her legs to give her some modesty.

"Jump, Grace; I will catch you," Vitus yelled up.

Grace looked behind her at the building. There were security cameras and barbed wire everywhere. Grace saw the door they had come out of and realized why Vitus had used it. It had a panel next to it that had had the wires ripped out of it, and it didn't look as if it was guarded. She couldn't go back that way. Looking forward from her vantage point, she could see trees everywhere. *Where am I?* Grace thought to herself. She looked down at the man below her and took a big breath. She had never trusted anyone this much before; could she do it? Closing her eyes, Grace leapt from the wall. The feeling of falling was freeing. It felt to her as if, for one moment, nothing really mattered. Her body came in contact with another as Vitus reached out to her and softened her landing. He stood her up and brushed the hair out of her face. "You can open your eyes now."

Grace opened her eyes and found she was looking straight into Vitus's crystal-blue orbs. If they had been in were a movie, this would have been the point where they kissed; but they weren't, and he lowered her to the ground and stood her up. Grace rearranged her clothing and started to walk. It didn't matter which direction she went in; she just needed to put as much distance between her and that facility as she could.

After they had been walking in an awkward silence for a while, Grace finally found her voice.

"So, Vitus, I have a few questions," Grace stated.

"You want to know what I am?" Vitus replied.

"No," said Grace. "I get that you are a vampire; you drank my blood, and you have fangs. Before I neurotically dug you up, I was actually searching for a werewolf, so the supernatural is not that new to me. What I do have a question about is why you killed all those men."

Vitus stopped walking and looked at Grace. "They were not human. I am not sure they were even alive to begin with. Vampires can sense a human presence over a mile away, but those things with the weapons were something else—something I have never encountered before."

Grace started walking again. *Not sure if they are even alive!* "Okay. With how strange my life has become in the last few weeks, I can actually believe that."

They walked in silence again. The crunch of the foliage under their feet seemed to echo throughout the woods. Grace looked over at her rescuer. He was built so big yet moved so gracefully. They had a long walk ahead of them, so she felt she might as well make more conversation.

"So how did you know I wasn't going to die when you fed off me?" Grace enquired.

Vitus looked a bit edgy at being asked this question. "I actually didn't," he ventured. "I thought I killed you. I had been imprisoned in that grave for such a long time, I was starved. When that first taste of blood hit my tongue, I became frenzied. It was only when I had drunk my fill that

I realized what I had done. I panicked and knew I had to get you somewhere to get help. I had to leave you outside that place, as my body hadn't finished regenerating yet, and I would have caused a stir if I had walked in." When Vitus finished talking, he looked at Grace as if he was waiting for a reaction.

Astonished by his answer, Grace did the only thing that any sane person would do—laugh hysterically. Her sudden outburst startled Vitus, and he stopped walking to make sure Grace was okay.

"I'm fine, really. Of course something like this would happen to me." Grace wiped the tears from her eyes. "I am so unlucky."

Once Grace had managed to compose herself, she asked the last burning question she had. "Given where you were buried and your age, how can you speak English so well?"

Vitus considered before answering. "When a vampire drinks the blood of a person, we can obtain his or her memories if we so wish. I must have done it instinctively, since I have been out of society for so long. It's a way to better prepare myself for the changes in time. Sometimes there are things we cannot control. That is how I learned English—from you. I also knew you were still alive, because about a day after I dropped you at the front of the hospital, I sensed you again. My kind can sense a person they have fed from for a while afterward. It is like an aura. If a vampire takes too much and kills the person being fed on, there is no aura any more. I was quite surprised when I felt your aura again after I was so sure I had killed you. That's when I realized you needed my help. Your aura had changed a bit, and there was an anxious feeling to it. Your blood has connected us briefly."

Out of all the things Vitus had just explained, there was only one thing that stood out "So you know all my memories?" Grace felt incredibly vulnerable, and she started to walk again so he wouldn't see her face.

"Yes, but I won't talk about it unless you want to." His voice sounded sad, which made Grace feel even more embarrassed.

"I'd rather not," said Grace quietly.

They continued to walk in silence again. *How unfair. He knows all about me, and I know nothing about him*, Grace thought to herself.

After they had been walking for a while, Grace's feet began to ache. "I need to rest for a bit," she said, leaning against a tree.

Vitus nodded and sat against a tree opposite Grace. Grace followed his cue and sat down and stretched out her legs. It wasn't the most comfortable seating arrangement, but she wasn't feeling fussy at the moment. She was just thankful for the rest. Grace glanced over at Vitus, who was gazing at her with a strange look on his face. She peered at the oversize shirt she was wearing, searching for what he was looking at. Vitus cocked his head as if he was listening to something. Grace strained her ears but could hear only the slight rustle of the tree leaves and the whistle of the wind. Vitus got to his feet and walked over to Grace and crouched down next to her.

"What—" Grace began.

"Shh!" said Vitus. He pulled Grace forward and put

his hand on her left shoulder blade. "Something is here—something that hums."

Grace thought for a second. "A bug!" She reached around to touch where Vitus's hand was and managed to feel a slight bump under her skin. "We need to get it out now!" Grace started to panic. She didn't want Dr. Werner to find them. The way he had looked at Vitus when he was taking out his men was unnerving, and she was pretty sure he wanted to acquire Vitus for his collection.

"I don't think it's an insect," said Vitus, frowning.

"Not that sort of bug! A tracker!" Grace exclaimed.

Vitus's face changed with the recognition of what it was. "What should I do? How do I remove it?" Vitus asked.

"I don't know, but it needs to happen now!"

Grace, foregoing any modesty, lifted the shirt off her back to give Vitus better access to the site.

"Stay still; this will hurt," said Vitus.

Grace prepared herself, and she felt a sharp pain. She bit down hard to prevent herself from yelling out.

"There, done," said Vitus. Grace turned to face him. He has holding an item in one hand that was covered in blood, and he was wiping his mouth with the other. Grace turned away so she could put the shirt back on, but she found she was having trouble with her left arm, as her back was still sore. She felt a pair of hands give her a hand to get back into the shirt.

"Thanks," said Grace.

Vitus cleaned the tracker on the singlet he was wearing and showed it to Grace. It was black and the size of a grain of rice.

"What should I do with this?" he asked.

Grace grabbed it and looked at the ground. She bent down and made a little hole in the ground, stuck it in there, and covered it up.

"If we destroy it, they will know we found it." Grace started to walk again. "We had better leave the area before we are found."

It was near dawn by the time they came across a town, and Vitus was feeling antsy. Apparently there was some truth to the myth about vampires and the sun. It starts to burn them instantly, and if they don't seek shelter quickly, they burn up completely. Grace was also feeling very tired and really wanted to rest. They walked around the outskirts of the town until they found a bush Grace could wait behind. Vitus was going to go into the town to seek shelter and to find Grace some proper clothes. Grace didn't approve of him stealing, but she did need better clothes to wear, and neither of them had any money. Vitus returned a short time later holding some bags. In them was some clothing that Grace could wear, a pair of shoes, and a facecloth with a bottle of water. He turned his back and allowed Grace to get changed and clean herself up. Removing the tracer chip had left quite a mess on Grace's back. They thought it would be best to get it cleaned up before they entered the town, so they didn't alarm the locals. Grace took the shirt that Vitus had given her off and dampened the cloth. She then attempted to clean her shoulder but found she couldn't quite reach. Covering herself with the new, clean shirt, she gave a cough. "I need help to clean my back."

Vitus turned around, keeping his eyes on the ground.

"It's okay, I am covered," said Grace, holding the shirt to

cover her. Vitus raised his eyes, and Grace handed him the cloth and turned around. His touch was gentle as he wiped the cloth over her. It wasn't just the cold air that brought gooseflesh to Grace's skin. He even cleaned the blood from the now faded pink marks that had been left on her arms from the tubes. When he was finished, Grace kept facing away from him and put the shirt on. The shirt and pants were a little too big for her, but the shoes fit all right. She just had to tie the laces a bit tighter.

"Done," said Grace as she turned to face Vitus.

Vitus smiled. "I found a place where we can sleep for the night. I checked the house out, and it looks as though the owner hasn't been home in a long time. The mail is building up, and the plants were stating to wilt."

Grace felt relieved. She was looking forward to sleeping in a bed, even if it was obtained by a little bit of breaking and entering.

They had to walk only a short distance to get to the house. Vitus was right; the letter box was full, and the plants were looking really thirsty. Grace looked down the street to make sure there were no neighbours about, but all she saw was darkened houses. As quickly and as quietly as they could, they ducked into the yard and went down the side of the house to get into the backyard. Vitus went to the back door and grabbed the door handle. With one quick jerk, the door handle broke and the door opened up. Grace made a mental note to get the house's address so she could send the occupants some money for repairs when she was reunited with her wallet.

Grace walked through the door and breathed a sigh of relief. She was looking around through the dark, trying to make out anything, when she realized Vitus hadn't followed her in. Grace turned around and saw Vitus standing just outside the doorway, looking apprehensive.

"What's wrong?" asked Grace.

"I need to be invited," replied Vitus, looking at the doorway.

"Oh, can I do it?" asked Grace.

"No, it needs to be the owner … unless …" He took a tentative step forward, inched his foot over the threshold, and exhaled in relief. "Must be a deceased estate."

"Oh," replied Grace. Even though she was relieved that Vitus could come inside, she was somewhat saddened by the thought. Maybe instead of sending a cheque, she would arrange for a repairman to come around and fix the lock.

"What would you have done if you couldn't get in?" asked Grace.

Vitus pointed to a shed in the backyard. "I would have given that a try."

Grace looked at the shed. It looked as if it could have done the job.

Vitus stepped forward and grabbed Grace's hand and led her further into the pitch-black house.

"I can see better in the dark than you can, and I don't want to turn any lights on," he whispered in Grace's ear. Hearing his voice that close to her ear, coupled with their skin-on-skin contact, gave Grace gooseflesh. Grace let herself be led further into the house. Vitus led her through a series of doorways until he stopped in a room. Grace's eyes were slowly adjusting to the dark, and she could make out Vitus's silhouette. She felt herself smiling but caught herself, knowing that he could see what she was doing.

"You can have this room, and I will sleep in the one next door." Vitus tried to let go of Grace's hand, but she held on.

"Stay in this room, please. I will feel much safer." Grace couldn't believe what had just come out of her mouth.

"As you wish, but I shall sleep on the floor," said Vitus.

"Are you sure you will be comfortable enough? That bed looks big enough for the both of us," Grace said, looking at the outline of the bed. She didn't want to be too forward, but she didn't want him to be uncomfortable after all he had done for her.

"After lying in that coffin for centuries, this carpeted floor will feel like clouds," replied Vitus.

Grace felt relived and disappointed at the same time. She wanted to be close to him, but not in *that* way. At least she thought so. She hadn't been this physically close to a male since Leonardo, and look how that turned out. She felt it was probably best she keep her distance.

Grace went over to the bed and shook the covers and sneezed. There seemed to be enough dust on them to fill a bucket.

"Bless you," she heard Vitus say.

"Thank you," replied Grace as she flicked the blankets a few more times. She crawled up onto the bed, took her shoes off, and shimmed under the blankets while Vitus went and got bedding from the next room. While she was under there, she removed her pants; she always had trouble sleeping with them on. Grace got herself comfy and looked towards the window which Vitus was standing in front of. He must have returned without Grace realizing it. Grace was looking at him when he began to remove his singlet. Even though it was dark, Grace could make out his body in the low light.

Oh my! She thought. He looked like one of the men she had seen posing for perfume ads, but bigger. His abs were well defined, and his chest was broad and smooth. Grace had never seen anything like it and had the ridiculous notion of rubbing her hands all over it. She was sorely disappointed when he then lay down on the floor. Grace realized that she was breathing heavily now and had to concentrate to get her breathing under control. *What has come over me! I barely know him!* Grace scolded herself internally.

After they had been lying in silence for a while, Grace could hear him tossing and turning on the floor. She cleared her throat and said in a voice unlike hers, "You are uncomfortable; you can sleep up here with … er … I mean next to me." Grace heard Vitus sigh as if he was giving in.

"Okay," he said stiffly.

Grace hurriedly shuffled over to give him plenty of room, and she then turned in the bed so she was facing away from him. She felt the bed dip on one side as he got into it, and then a breeze as he got under the blankets. Grace had the blankets right up under her chin, and she muttered, "Good night."

"Good night, Grace," Vitus returned.

"Thanks for saving me," Grace said

"Thank you for reviving me."

Grace forced herself to relax and not think of the big mass of a man lying next to her. She had never slept beside a male before, even when she was married to Leonardo.

CHAPTER 7

Grace was woken up by a scuffling next to her. She sat up and looked around, noticing that the early morning light had entered the room. The commotion that had woken her up was Vitus fleeing out of the bed and into a shadowed corner in the room. The curtains in the room they had fallen asleep in were not very good for blocking out the light, and poor Vitus was sleeping in its path. Grace could smell burnt flesh and saw that Vitus had a nasty-looking burn across his chest. She looked around the room and spotted a blanket that Vitus had brought into the room during the night. She got out of bed and dragged a chair over to the window. Grace then stood up and covered the window with the blanket, blocking out the sun's rays. Grace didn't even care that she wasn't wearing any pants. Her main concern was to help Vitus. As the room plunged in darkness, Grace heard a sigh of relief come from Vitus.

"Are you okay?" asked Grace to the darkness.

"I will be soon enough; thank you," replied Vitus in a strained voice.

By the look of that burn, Grace knew he must have been in immense pain. She felt her way back to the bed and got back in. After a while, Vitus joined her. He groaned and moved stiffly as he settled back into the bed.

"Is there anything I can do to take the pain away?" asked Grace. The idea of him being in pain made Grace feel uneasy.

"Just sleep, dear Grace," Vitus replied in a strained voice. "By dusk the burn will be barely there."

Grace covered herself up and got herself comfy. It didn't take long for her to hear the steady breathing of Vitus, indicating he had gone back to sleep. Grace lay there and listened to the steady rhythm of his breath. The only person she had ever shared a bed with was with Rose, back in the 1700s. In the earlier days, they didn't have much in the way of money or possessions, and they had to share a lot of things. Grace thought briefly of her marriage to Leonardo. They had never slept in the same bed together, so this was all new to her. As she thought about it more, sadness started to swell in Grace's chest. Determined not to shed a tear, she brought herself back to the now. She still had a long journey ahead of her and didn't need any distractions, and right now she was lying next to a beast of a man. Grace frowned. *Why the hell am I thinking like this?*

The next time Grace woke up, she was well rested. It took a few moments for her to realize there was a warm body lying right up against her. After a bit of stealthy head turning, Grace noticed that it was Vitus's back hard up against hers. She wasn't sure why he was warm, being dead and all, but she decided that she would ask him about it later. For now she would just secretly enjoy this moment.

It wasn't long until Vitus moaned and Grace felt him

roll away. She took the opportunity to stretch. Her body had a few aches and pains from walking so much the night before. Once her bones stopped cracking in protest, Grace decided that her tired muscles needed a nice, hot shower to loosen up. Sighing, Grace sat up. *May as well hunt down a towel and look for a shower*, she thought to herself.

"Good evening, Grace. Did you sleep well?" Vitus's voice came through the darkness still with a hint of sleepiness.

"Very well," Grace replied quietly, undergoing an uncharacteristic onset of shyness. "I'm going to take a shower and freshen up."

The room was quite dark, and Grace had to use her hands against the wall to navigate. She didn't want to try to turn on any lights, just in case they might alert the neighbours that someone was unlawfully camping out in the house. Grace awkwardly shuffled herself along the wall, hoping she wouldn't run into anything.

Vitus chuckled. "Do you need assistance?"

Grace sighed. She must have looked ridiculous. "Yes, please."

She heard him get off the bed swiftly and sensed him move over to her. He grabbed her hand and walked her through a doorway. Not wanting to walk in an awkward silence, Grace asked, "Why are you so warm?"

"It shows that I am well fed. When a vampire feeds, he or she temporarily warms up. This is when we are at our strongest. When body temperature drops, so does my strength, and my need for blood increases."

"So if you are stone cold, you are starving?"

"Precisely. Here is the bathroom."

They walked into a room, and Grace felt cold tiles under her feet. She then felt a towel brush against her.

"The cupboards are still stocked," said Vitus.

"Thank you," Grace replied as she gripped the towel. Grace played with the towel in her hands and waited until she heard Vitus leave the room. Once he left, she quickly got undressed and felt her way to the shower. She then found the taps and turned them both on and stepped in, dropping the towel on the floor within reach. After a few adjustments to the water temperature, Grace found a comfortable balance. She then submerged herself in the falling water. It was soothing and refreshing having the water run over her after the ordeals of the night before. So much had happened to her, and she had managed not to freak out.

Grace opened her eyes and noticed that a blue light had filled the bathroom. After rubbing her eyes a couple of times, she realized the light was real. Enough light was being emitted that she could now make out the features of the bathroom. Grace cut her shower short and turned off the water. She then groped along the floor until she found her towel in preparation to seek out the source of the light. Once out of the shower, it didn't take her long to find what was making the blue light. It was a bright blue rose sitting in the middle of the floor. Instead of feeling alarmed, Grace felt relieved. "Rose," she murmured to herself. She bent down and picked up the rose. It was absolutely radiant and oozed with magic. Surprisingly, it didn't make Grace feel uneasy, and she actually welcomed it. Grace gripped the towel tightly in one hand and the rose even tighter in the other, and she exited the bathroom.

The rose illuminated the house, so it made finding Vitus

easier. It was quite a nice house, actually. There were still photos hanging in frames on the wall, but Grace chose to ignore them. She realized that if they were still hanging up in a deceased estate, then the former owner must not have had any family left. Grace kept going, looking for Vitus. She found him in the bedroom, making the bed. He stopped what he was doing and looked up when Grace and the brightly lit rose entered the room.

"Rose!" said Grace, holding the rose out in front of her.

Vitus looked at the rose and then at her. "Yes, it is."

"No, I mean, I know it is a rose, but it is a message from my friend Rose. She is a witch," replied Grace. Her brow furrowed as she remembered their discussion while escaping. "You should know that if you gained my memories."

"Out of respect for you, I chose to shut them out," replied Vitus with a sincere look on his face.

Grace smiled. This man was so gentlemanly it almost diverted her attention from the rose. She shook her head to regain her focus. "It's a sign she is looking for me." Grace studied the rose and thought for a second, and then she walked over to the bedroom window and looked out. She wasn't completely sure what she was looking for, but she was sure she would know it when she saw it. Grace didn't see much at that window, so she went to a room that had a window facing the front yard.

"There!" Grace called out excitedly.

Vitus came over and stood close to Grace. Her heart skipped a beat when he brushed up against her arm. She tried to ignore it.

Grace pointed. "Over there, near the gate."

As brightly illuminated as the rose in Grace's hand,

there sat a single petal in the driveway of the house they were in. Grace stood on her toes and saw that there was another petal further in the street.

"If we follow those petals, we will find Rose," Grace said with certainty. She then moved to go towards the front door, but Vitus grabbed her arm.

"It's okay; I know it is her," Grace said.

"I know that," Vitus replied with an amused look on his face, "but you need to get dressed first."

After Grace had got herself decent in her "borrowed" clothes, she tidied up the house a bit and gave the garden a watering. While she was busy attending to the house, Vitus went out to get some supplies. By the time Vitus had returned, Grace had finished everything she had set out to do. Vitus showed her a tent and two sleeping bags that he had acquired. Grace pursed her lips and tried not to think about how he had acquired them, but it would make their travels so much easier. That and they wouldn't need to break into any more houses—even if they were deceased estates.

When they had finished packing all the supplies, they left the cottage. When they reached the gate, they could clearly see a trail of petals leading them down the street. Grace smiled. She was worried that Rose and Rhea wouldn't want anything to do with her after the way she had acted. Grace led the way down the path. Every petal she passed faded and disappeared in a small puff of smoke. Grace still clutched the rose she had found. It was her only link to her best friend. They followed the trail of petals out of the small town. Grace looked ahead and saw that the trail went on and on. She hoped that they wouldn't have to walk too far; she was in no shape for this type of exercise, and she was sure she was going to get huge blisters from her shoes.

Vitus and Grace talked through the whole night. It helped to pass the time and allowed them to get to know each other a bit more. Grace asked Vitus a lot of questions, as she had never met anyone that was older than her, so it was very exciting for her. It turned out he had been put in that grave by his own maker, whom he referred to as his sire. The vampire who had turned him thought him too much of a threat to keep around. Vitus's sire had plans of making a great vampire army that would bow to his every command and help him conquer countries and bring him a vast fortune. Vitus rebelled against him and was soon made an example of. His sire made his other recruits stake Vitus and bury him in that grave, dooming him to an eternity of purgatory. Grace was going to ask how she figured into it all, as she had dug him up, but she was too shy to ask. She changed the subject and decided to tell him about all the technology that was available now. He seemed quite impressed with smartphones and all the information they could access. Vitus was even more amazed about planes. When Grace told him they had ended up in Bulgaria, he didn't believe they had flown in on a plane. His face lit up in awe when she was explaining flying to him. His laughter and excitement were contagious, and soon Grace found herself marvelling at planes too.

As dawn was soon approaching, they decided to set up camp under the shade of a huge tree. In no time at all, they managed to set the tent up and roll the sleeping bags out. Grace was impressed with her work, as she had not been camping before and had managed to put in a good effort helping Vitus set up. He had never done anything like this before either, so they both were learning. They had brought a tarp along to throw over the tent as an extra precaution from the sun. Grace took off her shoes with a massive sigh, but she recoiled at the sight of her socks. Dirt had managed to get into her shoes, and her socks looked gross. Grace quickly took them off and tucked them into the shoes and put them outside the tent. She didn't want Vitus to smell them all night. Grace gave her feet a quick brush off with her hand and crawled inside the tent. She determined that if she ever had to do this again, she would be sure to bring baby wipes along to freshen up a bit. She crawled into her sleeping bag and started to dress down so she could get comfortable. Once settled, she stared up at the dark roof of the tent and waited. Now that she was inside the tent, she didn't feel very tired. Moments later Vitus joined her in the tent, bringing in a torch. He had already taken his shirt off outside and was putting on quite the unintentional display. Grace tried really hard not to stare, but it was next to impossible. She reluctantly forced herself to turn away as he got into his sleeping bag.

"Good night, Grace," Vitus said.

"Good night, Vitus," Grace replied. She heard him turn over, and within moments his breathing evened out and he was asleep. It didn't take long after that for Grace to fall into a deep sleep in which she dreamt of Vitus, minus his shirt.

Grace's slumber was disturbed by Vitus gently shaking her. "Grace, wake up; I think there is someone coming," Vitus said in a serious, hushed tone.

Grace's eyes opened up under protest. Vitus had turned a torch on. "Huh?" she replied. Moving her head, Grace noticed a distinctive dribble mark near where her mouth had been and quickly used her hand to cover it up. Vitus got up and went to the tent entrance. Grace listened hard but couldn't hear anything.

"Are you sure?" asked Grace, starting to feel a bit anxious. She hoped they hadn't been found by Dr. Werner already.

Vitus closed his eyes and then nodded. "Yes, definitely. I can hear someone coming this way. It could be more than one, though."

"Is it dark yet?" asked Grace. She wasn't sure how long they had been asleep for, and the tarp was very effective in keeping out the light. Vitus raised the zip a bit, and a beam of light came through the gap. Vitus took a step back and raised his eyebrows at Grace.

"I'll go out," Grace offered.

"Are you sure?" asked Vitus.

"Yeah, I don't want you getting burnt again," Grace replied, reaching for her pants. After a momentary pants dance in the sleeping bag, Grace was dressed and ready to go. Vitus got to the back of the tent to avoid the sunlight, and Grace unzipped the tent and exited. She stood at the entrance of the tent and took in her surroundings. The sun was low in the sky. She listened hard for a bit but still couldn't hear anything.

"Sunset will be soon," Grace yelled into the tent. She could tell this by the long shadows the trees surrounding them were casting. She heard Vitus reply, "Oh good."

Grace stood and listened for a bit longer, and soon

she could make out the distinctive sound of footsteps approaching. She turned in the direction of the incoming steps and started to head cautiously in that direction, praying the whole time it wasn't the doctor. A few minutes later, she heard some voices—female voices. Grace let out a sigh of relief, hoping they were just hikers that had gotten lost. As they got closer, Grace could hear them more clearly, and she recognized one of them.

"Rose!" Grace yelled out before she could even think.

The footsteps stopped as someone gasped "Grace?" a voice uttered.

Grace ran in the direction the voice had come from. After running a short distance, she saw a most welcome sight—Rose and Rhea walking with backpacks on, both wearing expressions of surprise. She sprinted as fast as she could towards the duo and nearly knocked Rose to the ground when she approached her. Gripping Rose in a tight embrace, Grace felt tears stream down her face, and she let them run freely.

"I am so sorry!" she said, gripping her friend.

"Shh, it's okay," said Rose soothingly, and she hugged Grace back.

Grace finally let go of Rose and turned to Rhea. "I have no idea what came over me when I took your car. I am sorry for how I acted; I hope you forgive me?"

"There is nothing to forgive. Destiny was calling you," Rhea said with a wink.

Rose turned and looked at Rhea, who gave her an innocent look along with a shrug.

"I am so sorry it took us so long to find you. After you took off, we went back to Rhea's house to wait for you there.

It wasn't until we got a phone call informing us that Rhea's car was located at a cemetery that we got worried," Rose explained. "We went to the cemetery to get her car, hoping you would be nearby. When we got there, there was no sign of you at the car, so we decided to walk around the cemetery. While walking, we saw some policemen surrounding an old grave that had been freshly dug up. We got as close as we could so we could eavesdrop on the officers. They were saying that there was blood at the scene and that it may be connected to a Jane Doe that had been dropped off at the hospital. That's when we put two and two together. We went to the hospital to see if we could view your body. We made it all the way to the morgue before a doctor steered us away, claiming we had made a mistake. He seemed odd, but we left anyway; that's when we decided to use a tracking spell. It led us to an area in Hungary. We couldn't get an exact location, so I decided to try the Rose spell that led you to us. It wasn't until last night that it was successful. When you picked up the rose, all the rose petals started to glow. That's when I knew we would find you."

Grace hugged Rose again. "Oh, Rose! Don't feel sorry! Everything is all right now."

When they broke apart, Grace noticed that Rose was looking at something behind Grace. She turned around to see what she was looking at and saw Vitus standing a few feet behind her. He looked tired still, and a bit awkward.

"Oh yeah, this is Vitus. He saved me," said Grace, blushing.

"Oh my! A vampire!" Rhea said excitedly.

Rose looked Vitus up and down and then extended her hand "Pleased to meet you," said Rose, shaking his hand.

She then turned to Grace and said "What do you mean by 'saved'?"

"It is a very long story, and I will fill you in, but first we need to pack up our camp and get as far away from here as we can."

It didn't take them long to pack up Vitus and Grace's little camp. Rhea had thankfully driven her car there and had parked it a short distance away. Grace could have kissed the car when she saw it again. Her feet were in agony from walking for so long. When they got in, Grace felt embarrassed at the memory of stealing the car.

"I am really sorry I stole your car," said Grace to Rhea before they took off.

Rhea turned around in the driver's seat and looked at Vitus and Grace in the back seat. "It is fine; you can't fight these things," she said with a smile.

Grace blushed and turned to look out the window, pretending to take in the scenery. She could feel Vitus's eyes on her and tried to hide her smile.

While they drove, Grace filled the two witches in on everything. Rose cursed loudly when Grace told her about Dr. Werner's experiments. When she was telling them about the drowning experiment, Vitus grabbed onto Grace's hand and didn't let go. Grace really appreciated it; even though she felt safe with him, retelling the tale was hard.

"We need to find the werewolf and warn him," said Grace.

"We need to find the doctor and make him bleed," replied Rose through gritted teeth.

Grace raised her eyebrows in shock. Rose had never talked like that before.

"I agree," said Vitus. His jaw was tense, as if he was holding something in.

"Look; what happened to me was bad, but I really am okay," Grace said. "I am more worried about others that are stuck in that facility or others that could get caught. I really think we should find this werewolf as quickly as we can, and then figure out what to do about Dr. Werner."

"I agree with Grace," said Rhea. "He already said he was looking for the werewolf, and I would hate for him to get his hands on it. We have a few weeks until the next full moon, so we have time to get organized. Hopefully we can get to the wolf before the doctor does."

"I may be able to help," offered Vitus. He had been quiet for most of the drive, and Grace's ears pricked up when she heard his voice. "Being a vampire, I can sense other supernatural beings. Finding the werewolf will be no problem at all for me. If you will allow it, I would like to help you for as long as you will have me."

"That would be fantastic!" said Rose.

Grace silently agreed. She wasn't ready to let Vitus go just yet.

CHAPTER 8

The drive back to Bulgaria was mostly uneventful. They had to do all their travelling at night for Vitus's sake, so they found a place to stay before the sun came up. The three girls shared a room, while Vitus got to have a room to himself, much to Grace's disappointment—not that she let anyone know. The most exciting part of the trip was letting Vitus out just before the boarders so he could find a different way to get around the security. Once they had passed through, they found him a couple of miles up the road and picked him up again. Rose had thought ahead and brought along Grace's passports and wallet so she could pass through. Unfortunately, Vitus didn't have anything, but Rose said that once they got back to Rhea's, she would contact her documents guy and see if he would make some IDs for Vitus and send them express. It seemed that Vitus might be hanging around for some time, and having an identity would make that much easier for him. Knowing that he was going to be around for a while longer thrilled Grace. She liked having him around.

They made it back to Rhea's house in no time at all. When they got there, Rhea invited Vitus in straight away.

She almost bubbled over with excitement as the vampire crossed over the threshold. She felt they might as well stick together since he was going to help them out.

As Rhea was giving him the tour, she stopped dead in her tracks and looked at Vitus. "I haven't got another room," she said apologetically.

"That is okay; I am quite happy to sleep on the couch or on the floor," Vitus replied. They had brought all their camping equipment with them. "I am sure I will be comfortable enough. It is certainly better than my previous bed." He chuckled.

Grace had the urge to tell him that he could share her bed with her, but she held her tongue. Rhea must have sensed her intentions and gave her a secret smile. Grace tried to keep her face straight, but she knew Rhea would be able to sense her emotions. Grace quickly thought of a getaway plan and faked a yawn. She bid everyone good night and retreated to her room. Grace reached her room and laid out on the bed, dirty clothes and all. Truth was, she was exhausted, both mentally and physically. She had had a big couple of days. To start with, there had been the frenzied digging up of a grave and then getting drained by a corpse. That she could easily get over. If she had to, she would save Vitus all over again. Then there had been the ordeal with the doctor. She had never been experimented on before, and had never been held captive, and she wasn't sure how she was to feel about that. Then there was her rescuer, Vitus. She was not sure what to make of him. He was insanely handsome, and they seemed to have some sort of connection. Every time she was in his presence, it felt right; it felt like home. She had never had this with

Leonardo. With Leonardo, it was all about having children and making the right impressions and befriending the right people. Now that she thought about it, her marriage had been more of a business contract than a love affair. It had seemingly been her job to be his wife. Whatever she thought love was, was obviously not, even if she had wanted it to be. Thinking of her past made started to make her feel annoyed, so she started to think of the doctor and about what he had said about her. She had never thought herself as having anything special before; she had thought of herself only as cursed. She supposed immortality may appeal to some people, but it did not appeal to her. It had brought her nothing but trouble. However, since meeting Vitus, she hadn't been sure how she felt about immortality any more.

A knock on Grace's door disrupted her train of thought. "Come in," she said, rising to her elbows so she could see who was coming through the door.

Rose's head peered through the door, her face displaying her trademark smile. "Hi, I was just seeing how you were doing?"

"I am fine. Just really tired," replied Grace.

Rose walked into the room and sat on the bed with her legs crossed.

"You sure you don't want to talk about Dr. Werner some more? That was pretty intense," Rose said, looking at Grace with concern in her eyes.

Grace looked at her friend and noted concern in her face. "I'm good. No permanent damage. Nothing a tub of ice cream and a cheap chick flick cannot fix."

Rose smiled. "That's easily fixed!"

"But not tonight. I am tired, and I don't think I could

stay awake long enough to get through the opening scenes of a film," replied Grace.

"Fair enough. Want to talk about Vitus then?" Rose tested with a girly grin.

"What do you mean?" Grace asked innocently while avoiding Rose's eyes.

"Come on, Grace. It's the first time ever I get to have girl talk with you; you cannot clam up on me."

Grace couldn't help but smile. "What about him?"

"Well, I've seen the way you guys look at each other when you think no one is looking. It is exciting!" Rose all but squealed the last part of that sentence.

Grace laughed. "Okay, he is handsome and has something about him that I can't explain, but it's not like something can come of it."

"Why not?" asked Rose. "You are both immortal."

Grace opened her mouth to talk, but she couldn't think of anything to say.

"I will leave you to sleep," said Rose with a wink. She got up, gave Grace a smile, and left.

Yeah right! Like I will be able to sleep now! Grace thought to herself. Deep down, she knew she had feelings for Vitus, but she wasn't sure what those feelings meant yet. They were both immortal, so outliving each other wasn't an issue. The only issue Grace had was that she was terrified. She was scared of getting hurt again—scared of that empty feeling she got in her chest when she thought of Leonardo and his betrayal. Sure, this was different. She didn't have a younger, more fertile sister living with her to replace her with. That last thought brought Grace's thoughts to a halt. She hadn't thought of her sister in a long time. She never wondered about what Marion's life was like with Leonardo. Did they have children? Did she ever miss Grace? How did Leonardo explain her sudden disappearance? Whatever happened, she just hoped that he was a lot nicer to her than he had been to Grace. Staring at a wall, Grace felt a tear roll down her cheek, and she wiped it away with the back of her hand. She took a big breath and thought of a new resolve. She was not going to be scared of new things, even if one of those new things was love.

The next morning, Grace woke up early. It was the first time in a long time that she had dreamt of her sister. Once she had woken up from her dream with her heavily pregnant sister in it, she wasn't keen on going back to sleep to continue it. Grace threw back the blankets and got up out of bed. She showered, dressed, and headed for the kitchen, thinking she might as well get started on some breakfast. As Grace was frying up some eggs, her eyes kept wandering over towards the lounge door. Her curiosity was burning deep in her, so she decided to chance a peek. Slipping off her shoes so she could sneak quietly, Grace tiptoed over to the door carefully. Feeling all stealthy, she leaned up against the door and listened hard for any sounds of movement from within. Not hearing anything, she put her hand on the door handle and slowly turned it, holding her breath. The handle turned quietly, and Grace let out a sigh of relief. She then pushed the door slightly and silently cursed at the squeak the protesting hinges let out. Having gone too far to back out now, Grace was determined to keep on going. She opened up the door enough to poke her head through. The room was completely blacked out, and Grace couldn't see anything. In the dark, she could hear Vitus breathing. Feeling disappointed at not having seen him physically, Grace pulled her head out from the doorway and closed the door quietly again. She smiled at the door and silently celebrated her little victory. She had managed to pull off her little peeping Tom mission without waking him up. Grace turned around, and her happy expression quickly turned into big doe eyes. Standing at the stove, getting eggs out of a pan, was Rhea in her dressing gown.

"Good morning," said Rhea with her eyebrows raised up high and displaying a knowing smile. "Did you sleep well?"

"Er, yes, good morning. I slept really well, thank you," Grace replied, feeling her face reddening. "I was just, umm … I mean, I was just …"

"Do you like your eggs runny?" Rhea asked, holding the spatula in her hand.

"Um, yes, thank you," replied Grace. Rhea dished out the eggs and made some toast. Once it was all ready, they sat at the table and started to eat breakfast. Grace watched Rhea apprehensively and started to think up excuses in her head.

"So when Rose wakes up, I think we should discuss what to do next," Rhea said between bites of toast

Oh thank god! Grace thought, relieved, as Rhea kept talking about the day ahead. She had no idea how she was going to explain her little spy exhibition.

Once Rhea and Grace had finished their breakfast, they made themselves some coffee and went outside to Rhea's veranda to discuss what they should do next. They decided to let the others catch up on sleep; they deserved it.

"We have a fortnight until the next full moon. Rose has

everything she needs for the tracking spell except for the DNA, so we can't use it yet. Hopefully we can find some soon." Rhea took a sip of her coffee. Her face screwed up in concentration.

"What about Vitus?" Grace asked.

Rhea looked at Grace quizzically; then her eyes opened in realization. "Oh, yes! With everything that has happened," she said excitedly.

"I had forgotten what he had said! He can sniff out the werewolf!" Grace chuckled at her enthusiasm. "Yeah. He could try to do some tracking before the full moon. Could save us a bit of trouble."

"Good idea. The quicker the better. I don't like the idea of Dr. Werner hanging around. There are too many supernatural beings in the area, and I would hate for him to get his hand on another innocent."

"Other supernatural beings?" Grace asked.

Rhea looked at Grace amusedly. "I keep forgetting how new to this you are. There are supernatural beings everywhere, but they tend to stick to the same area. Makes it easier to hide."

Grace nodded and then asked. "What is around here— other than witches and werewolves?"

"Well, we have fairies, banshees, mages, and I have even met a troll a few towns over," replied Rhea.

"Oh," Grace said, feeling naive.

"All supernatural beings have managed to adapt over time, making concealment easier," said Rhea. "It is quite easy for me, because I am a witch. I'm human with special powers. Unfortunately, it is not as easy for beings like trolls and banshees. They kind of stand out."

Grace's mind was blown. She had never known how vast the world was. She was getting curious.

The sound of the door broke her train of thought, and Rose walked out holding a plate of food and a mug. She must have grabbed some of the leftovers that Grace had left on the stove. Rose walked over to the porch step and sat down.

"Morning, Rose," said Grace

"Morning. Mmm, this breakfast smells good," said Rose, looking at her food eagerly.

"We were just discussing what to do next," said Rhea. Rose nodded and started on her food as Rhea continued. "I know you still need some DNA for the spell, but in the meantime, we were going to ask Vitus to help us out by tracking him."

Rose swallowed what was in her mouth and looked at Grace with a grin. "I can't see him saying no."

Grace blushed, and Rhea giggled. "Me neither," Rhea added.

They spent the next half hour chatting about their plans; then they moved inside to the kitchen to wash up the dishes. While they were in there, the lounge room door opened and Vitus walked through. His hair was still messed up from sleep, and his eyes still had a tired look to them.

"Good morning, ladies. Did you all slept well?" asked Vitus.

Grace replied before she realized the words had left her mouth. "Good morning! Yes, we did."

"That's good." Vitus gave her a warming smile.

"We were talking about you earlier," Rose said.

"All good things, I trust?" replied Vitus.

Grace nodded. She didn't trust anything that would come out of her mouth.

"We were talking about your offer to help us with our werewolf problem," Rhea said.

"Have you decided to accept my help?" Vitus asked.

"Yes, it will give us a head start," replied Rhea.

"I will be happy to help in any way I can. I see it is still light out, so I will start after sundown," Vitus said.

"Actually, I think I have a solution for your sun problem," said Rhea excitedly. She got up and disappeared through the doorway towards the bedrooms. Vitus watched her leave with interest and then looked at Grace.

Grace was aware of his stare and started to fiddle with her hair. "So what do werewolves smell like?" she asked, hoping to fill the silence with some form of chatter.

"It is hard to explain. Imagine the smell of a normal dog, but thicker," replied Vitus.

Grace thought a moment. "I have no idea what that would smell like," she chuckled.

Thankfully Rhea returned and the awkwardness stopped.

"Here. I have had this in my collection for a long time, and I think we all agree that you should have it." Rhea indicated for Vitus to hold out his hand, to which he obliged. Rhea dropped the item she had in her hand, and Grace watched Vitus's expression change to one of awe. Vitus's eyes opened wide as he held the ring up to the light. "Can it be?"

"What is it?" enquired Grace.

"It's the ring of Astrum—the ring of the sun," replied Vitus with wonder in his voice.

"That's nice," said Grace. She had no idea what that meant.

"It means that Vitus can go into the sun without getting hurt," replied Rose. "I have only read about them. They are really rare, and to see one is amazing! I wonder if it actually works."

"There is only one way to find out," said Vitus. He slipped the ring onto his ring finger and flexed his fingers a few time. He then walked towards the front entrance. Grace got off her seat and followed him out. She found him staring at the front door as if it were a huge hurdle. With a deep breath, Vitus reached out and turned the handle, opening the door, and took a tentative step out into the sunlight. Grace held her breath, praying that it would work. She watched as he flinched at first and then raised his hands to shield his eyes. Vitus took a few steps out and then stopped. His sudden laughter made Grace jump. She watched him move his arms out to his sides. The smile on his face was infectious. He looked up into the sun and smiled. "It has been a very long time since I felt the warmth of the sun upon my face." His voice sounded almost sad.

Grace stepped outside and stood next to him. As selfish as it sounded, she wanted to be close to him in this moment.

Vitus looked down at her as she approached. His eyes were running over her face as if he were seeing her for the first time. "I thought you looked beautiful in the moonlight, but seeing you in the sunlight for the first time is a sight I will never forget." Grace smiled and blushed. "I am sorry," said Vitus. "That was a bit inappropriate of me."

"No," said Grace, boldly reaching out and grabbing Vitus's hand. "It is perfectly fine."

Vitus pulled Grace into his arms and looked deeply into her eyes. With their eyes locked, he brought her face up to his. Grace's heart started to race; she knew what was about to happen. This was going be her first kiss in centuries, and she hoped she wouldn't stuff it up.

Grace closed her eyes as Vitus brought their faces together, and in a moment their mouths met. The contact nearly made Grace gasp, but she didn't want to break the kiss. Not yet. His kiss was passionate and careful, yet powerful. She had never felt anything like it before, and she felt something stir in her she had never felt before. She reached around Vitus's back and brought him in closer, getting lost in the kiss—in the moment. His body felt warm up against her, and yet she still didn't feel close enough to him.

Grace heard a squeal behind her and broke off the kiss. She turned toward the sound and noticed Rose standing in the doorway of the house. She had her hands to her mouth and was bouncing on the spot. "I knew it, I knew it, I knew it!"

Grace blushed and tried to hide her face in Vitus's shirt while he just laughed.

"Oh! Don't mind me. Pretend I'm not even here," said Rose, beaming.

Yeah, right! thought Grace. She removed her face from Vitus's shirt and looked up at him. He was radiant, and the look in his eyes nearly made Grace weak at the knees. She could look into his eyes for eternity.

After enjoying the sun for a few moments, Grace and Vitus went back inside. Although she felt she could have stayed in Vitus's arms forever, they had a job to do. They had to find the werewolf before Dr. Werner did. They entered the kitchen and noticed Rhea had spread out her maps on the table. She was leaned over them with a pen in her mouth, deep in thought, while Rose was busy studying a book. Not wanting to disturb them, they chose two seats on the opposite side of the table and quietly sat down.

Grace sat next to Vitus and started to study the new marks Rhea had made on the map. While trying to make heads and tails of what Rhea had done, she felt Vitus grab her hand. She looked away from the map and glanced at Vitus and smiled broadly.

"I knew this would happen," Rhea's voice cut in. "Your souls have been looking for each other for a long time."

Vitus nodded and looked at Grace. "That makes sense. While I was in purgatory, I dreamt of you. I didn't know who you were, but somehow it felt as if I knew you."

Grace thought for a moment and remembered her dreams. "As odd as this sounds, I had dreams of the grave you were buried in. But they didn't start until I entered the country."

"Destiny can only reach so far," said Rhea. "If you had had the dreams while you were back in America, it would have made it too easy."

"When we find this werewolf, I will have to thank him or her for bringing you to me," Vitus said while giving Grace's hand a little squeeze.

Grace blushed. She felt everyone's eyes on her and needed a distraction, as she wasn't used to the attention.

"Speaking of the werewolf, what do we do now?" Grace asked, hoping to divert the attention away from her.

"Well, I can start walking through the streets to see if I can pick up a scent," said Vitus.

"Good idea. I can show you on the map the most frequented areas to make it easier," said Rhea eagerly.

"I will start right away," said Vitus with determination.

Grace was unsure of what she could do and said the first thing that came to her mind. "I might go for a jog."

Three faces turned to look at her with confusion. Apparently what she had said was enough to pull Rose's attention from her book.

"I have had to escape a facility from which a mad doctor wants to harvest my blood and conduct all sorts of experiments on me. I am also hunting a werewolf—a supernatural creature that up until recently I thought was a myth. I need to get fit and learn how to defend myself. If I end up getting captured again, I don't want you guys coming in to rescue me and getting caught yourselves. In saying that, I am going to have to go back to that facility eventually to shut it down. That may seem heroic of me, but I can't die, so I am a good candidate to get it done, and I can't get it done while being so unfit."

The trio looked at her with a deafening silence. Grace looked at them, waiting for someone to say something. Rose was the first to speak up.

"Grace, I love you, but you are dumb. We will never let you fight alone." That was followed by nods of agreeance from Rhea and Vitus. Grace smiled. She had never felt so loved.

After jogging every day for a week, Grace could already feel the improvement. The first night, she had barely made it two blocks before she had to stop. Now she could do three. Hey, any improvement is better than none!

Grace had just returned from her jog when she found Vitus, Rose, and Rhea talking excitedly around the kitchen table. Wanting to know what they were discussing, Grace walked up to the trio while using a towel to dry off her perspiration. Vitus turned around as she approached, and smiled at her. "Hello, sweet Grace. Did you have a good run?"

Grace smiled. She still wasn't used to the pet names yet. "Yes I did, thank you. What is going on?"

"Vitus has picked up on the werewolf's scent," said Rhea excitedly.

"Indeed I have had some luck. I should be able to locate him tomorrow," said Vitus.

"Oh good!" replied Grace, grateful that there had finally been some progress. During the last week, Vitus had been out of the house most of the time, searching, while Grace struggled through jogging and workout DVDs. Unlike her name, she wasn't very graceful.

"I traced the scent to a mechanical workshop. I could smell him everywhere there."

"Him?" asked Grace.

"Yes. Once I picked up on his scent, I could tell straight away."

"That will make it so much easier to find the person," said Rhea.

"Rhea and Vitus will take the car to the shop tomorrow and see if they can find him. After getting some details, they will return, and then we can decide how to approach him," said Rose. "We will need to be careful not to spook the poor guy."

Easier said than done! Grace thought to herself, knowing that being told you are different isn't always an easy pill to swallow.

"We can relax the rest of the day," said Rhea.

"Okay, good idea," said Grace.

"Oh, not you two. You guys are going to go on a date," said Rose with a big smile.

"Pardon?" asked Grace.

"It was my idea. I want to take you on a date, as Rose told me it is called," said Vitus.

"Oh," replied Grace, completely surprised. "Where are we going?"

"On a picnic. Rhea has told me of a place we can go. She said it is a beautiful spot that not many people know about."

Grace stood there blankly, wondering what she should do. She had never been on a date before.

Rose leaned over and whispered to her, "Go have a shower. I laid out some clothes for you on your bed."

Right. Shower, clothes—good start. Grace turned and went to her room to get ready.

After she had finished showering and dressed, she stood in front of the mirror, looking at her reflection. She had no idea what do to with her hair. It had been a while since she really cared about what she looked like. Her medium-length brown hair hung limp around her shoulders, almost as if it were mocking her. Rose had picked out a flowing red dress that went to her knees. She decided against the heels but chose some flats instead, just in case they had to do a bit of walking.

A knock broke Grace's concentration. "Come in," she said, pulling her eyes away from her reflection.

Rose entered the room with a beauty case in hand. "Need help?" she said, raising the bag.

Grace could have kissed her. She was no good at this girly stuff. She had given it all up when she came to America. She didn't have the urge to be a lady after all she had been through. Rose walked over to the bed and tipped out the beauty case. There were all sorts of items in there, from makeup to hair products; it was packed. She looked at Grace quizzically. "Hmm, wavy—definitely wavy." She picked up a hair-waving wand and plugged it into the wall outlet. "While that warms up, let's do your face. You don't need much done. Minimal is the way to go. We just want to highlight your features."

Grace didn't reply. She knew Rose wasn't talking to her. She was thinking out loud.

After being painted and sprayed and having her hair played with until it was stiff, Rose was satisfied. "There!" she said, taking a step back to allow Grace to see herself in the mirror. Grace took a deep breath and looked at her reflection. She had to admit Rose had done a top job. The makeup wasn't heavy, and even though her hair felt flammable, it looked natural, and Rose had managed to cover up her scar.

"Rose, thank you," said Grace, embracing her friend.

"It's nothing. Now go have fun; we have kept him waiting for long enough."

Grace took one last look at her reflection and took a deep breath. *Here goes nothing!*

Grace met Vitus by the front door. He looked striking.

He was wearing a casual blue buttoned shirt and black slacks. What topped off his whole look was the way his face changed when he saw her. He smiled handsomely at her. "You look radiant."

Grace smiled back. "Thank you. Rose did all the work."

"I did nothing," said Rose from behind her. "You two go and have some fun."

Rhea passed Grace her car keys. "You are going to have to drive. Vitus doesn't know how to yet, but he knows how to get there."

"Rhea made me memorize the map," said Vitus with a smile.

Rhea passed Vitus a picnic basket. She caught a whiff of the food inside. It smelt good.

Grace and Vitus walked out the door and headed to the car. When they got there, Vitus held the driver's side door open for her.

"Thank you," she said, sliding in. She waited for Vitus to slide in next to her before she turned the car over and drove out of the driveway.

Vitus's directions led them out of town a bit and then down a small road. He directed her to pull up a few miles down the road. "We have to walk a bit, and then we are there," said Vitus.

Vitus grabbed the basket, and Grace locked the car. They walked hand in hand up a small hill. When they got to the top, the view took Grace's breath away. The surroundings were beautiful. They were at the top of a hill that overlooked a valley. There was a small creek flowing down the bottom of the hill, and wild flowers were growing everywhere. Vitus put the basket down and stood behind Grace and wrapped his arms around her. Between the embrace and the view, Grace would never forget this moment. She winced as her stomach gave a little growl and ruined the moment.

"Let's get some food into you," said Vitus, amused.

Vitus released his embrace and grabbed the blanket from the top of the basket. He flicked it a few times to unfold it and spread it on the ground. Grace watched his powerful arms the whole time. When it was spread out, Grace awkwardly sat down on the blanket, keeping her legs tucked underneath her. Vitus sat down next to her and proceeded to take the food out of the basket. Grace could tell that Rose had cooked the food. Having lived with Rose most of her life, Rose knew her style. Vitus must have sensed that she knew. "Rose cooked it all. I don't know how to cook." He seemed to be embarrassed.

"That's okay. I can teach you if you want," Grace offered.

Vitus smiled a boyish grin that melted Grace's heart. "I would very much like that."

They made it back to Rhea's house just after dark. Grace had such a wonderful evening she didn't want it to end. It could have hailed on them while they were eating, and it still would have been a great night.

They let themselves into Rhea's house, and Vitus went to put the picnic basket away. Grace walked into the lounge room, and a pair of heads turned around on the couch.

"Had a good evening?" Rose said with a smile on her face.

Grace smiled. "Yes I did. Thank you, both of you."

"It was mostly Vitus's idea," Rose said. "He wanted to do something special for you. Rhea and I jumped at the idea.

You deserve happiness, Grace; you really do. You may not realize it, but you have spent centuries moping. You have been surviving, not living, and you need to live."

Grace thought on that a bit. Rose was right. Sure, she had done the day-to-day things, such as going to work, paying bills, and going on the occasional touristy holiday, but she could not remember a time when she had been truly content. She could not remember a time when she had been happy or at peace—until today. During her date with Vitus, she had just laughed and lived in the moment. There had been no hidden thoughts of Leonardo, and no dwelling on her long life.

Grace noticed Rose get up off the lounge and come over to her. Rose spread her arms and gave Grace a big embrace. Grace hugged back and felt a tear run down her face. She didn't even know she was crying. Once she started, she couldn't stop. It was like a weight being lifted off her shoulders. All the emotions she had held in over the years were coming out in waves of wet sobs.

Once Grace was all cried out, she was exhausted and congested but felt better. She tried to use the back of her hand to clean up her face, but it was too much. A handkerchief appeared in front of her face, and she grabbed it. Rhea was standing on the other end of it, giving a worried but polite smile. Grace accepted it and proceeded to clean herself up. Rose released her, and Grace stood for a second and admired her friend. Rose was an amazing person; she always knew what Grace needed. Grace was determined to one day find a way to thank her.

"Vitus tried to come in, but I shooed him away," said

Rhea. "You needed to let it all out. If he had been here, you wouldn't have been able to let go."

Grace nodded. She didn't think she would be able to ugly-cry around him yet.

After confirmation that she didn't look messy, Grace went into the kitchen. Vitus was sitting at the table with a worried look on his face. He stood up when she entered the room.

"Are you okay?" Vitus asked.

"I am fine," said Grace. It was the first time in a long time that she actually meant it.

CHAPTER 9

Vitus and Rhea were on their excursion to the mechanic's while Rose and Grace sat at home watching TV. They were watching a documentary on the paranormal to kill some time.

"So since the supernatural world is real, do you think the paranormal is real too?" asked Grace

"Highly likely. Given our recent experiences, I am starting to seriously re-think Santa Clause," replied Rose "I may look in to it," she said with a decisive look on her face.

Not something else! thought Grace. "Sounds interesting." Grace secretly hoped that Rose wouldn't dig too deep into it. They had enough on their plate to deal with as it was.

They had nearly finished watching the show when Vitus and Rhea walked through the door. Grace got off the couch and greeted Vitus with a hug and quick kiss.

"How did it go?" she asked when they broke apart.

"Great. We have accurately identified the werewolf," Vitus said with his arm around Grace.

"Yeah, even I got a vibe from him," said Rhea. "His name is Gregori, and he works there as a mechanic and bookkeeper. After doing some probing, we found out he will be staying back late tonight to sort out the books. I think that would be a good time to go there and talk to him. That way we won't have any interruptions."

"Sounds good. Will we need anything?" asked Grace.

"I don't think so, but I think we should all go. He may need some convincing," said Rhea.

Grace nodded. She wasn't sure what she could do to convince him, but she supposed being there in body would be a start.

Later that evening, they were standing outside the mechanic's office, getting ready to go in. After a few glances at each other, they walked towards the door in silence. There wasn't really a conversation to go with the situation. Rose was out in front and reached the door first. She tried to turn the handle but found it was locked. She sighed, closed her eyes, and whispered "apertus." Grace heard a click, and then Rose turned the handle again. This time the door opened. Grace was quite impressed. They walked through the door into a reception area. Grace looked around the room to check out her surroundings. There was a high desk, a couch to sit on, and a table filled with out-of-date magazines. Grace closed the door behind her with a not-so-quiet bang. Grace winced at the sound and whispered, "Sorry."

Rhea just raised her hand as if to say "That's okay." Through the silence, they heard someone from a back room yell out. Rhea yelled a reply back. After a moment, Grace heard a chair scrape across the ground, followed by some approaching footsteps. A man in his late twenties came to the counter with a confused look on his face. Rhea stepped up to the counter and started talking to him. They decided it would be best for Rhea to do all the talking, since she was the only one that could speak Bulgarian. Gregori, as was written on his dirty work overalls, had a frown on his face as Rhea was talking to him. Once Rhea had stopped talking, she looked at him expectantly. After a moment of silence, he started to laugh.

Rhea turned to the rest of the group. "As expected, he doesn't believe me."

"He just needs some convincing then," Rose said with determination. She turned to the well-worn couch near the window and put her hands in front of her. The couch started to quiver, and then it rose off the ground. Gregori's eyes widened, and he started to talk really fast and point to the door.

"He is saying we can't fool him with magic tricks, and he wants us to leave. He said he has a lot of work to do and hasn't got time for pranks," said Rhea.

Vitus stepped forward wearing a smirk on his face. "My turn then."

He opened his mouth, and his canines elongated to become fearsome fangs. If Grace hadn't seen this before, she would have run out of the shop quick smart.

The poor mechanic raised his voice now and pointed to the door with more urgency.

"He really wants us to leave," said Rhea disappointedly.

Grace could see that the man was getting really agitated and thought it was probably best they did leave. "Maybe we should," she voiced out loud.

Rose set the couch back down, and the group filed out the door, going outside. When the door closed behind them, Grace heard the couch being moved across the floor. She assumed he must have moved it in front of the door to try to keep them out. They walked back to Rhea's car and got in.

"What did you say to him?" asked Grace from the back seat.

"I told him who we are and what we are. He laughed as if it were some kind of joke. I then told him what he was and started to go through what he would have been experiencing. I told him that there would have been nights when he blacked out and didn't remember a thing. Sometimes he would have up at home, but other times he would have woken up out of town or in a yard somewhere. When I told him that, he started to freak out a bit. I think he saw some truth in what I was saying but was too scared to believe me," Rhea replied.

"Well, plan B then," said Rose.

Plan B meant that Vitus was going to track him until the full moon. They would then try to approach him one more time just before he turned, hoping that they could convince him one last time. If he still didn't believe them, they were going to tranquillize him and record his transformation to show him the next day. It wasn't the best plan, but it was all they had; and they didn't have the luxury of time, what with Dr. Werner being in the area.

Vitus tracked Gregori's every move right up until the day before the full moon. He didn't want to lose track of him after they had just found him, and he was also making sure that Dr. Werner didn't find him first. That meant that Grace didn't get to see him that much, so she kept herself occupied by working out and practising shooting with a BB gun. She wanted to make sure she was fit and ready. She also wanted to be able to make a decent shot if she had to. She didn't have any sort of supernatural ability to add to the group, so she had to make herself feel useful somehow. When Rhea had found out how inadequate Grace felt, she had nearly broken down in tears. She gave Grace a huge hug and reassured her that she was as vital to the team as everyone else was. Grace appreciated the gesture but still wasn't convinced.

When the night finally came to talk to Gregori again, they were all ready to go. They had been preparing for weeks and were all geared up. Each had packed some strong chains, a video camera, blankets, and a few extra tranquilliser darts, just in case. They thought it best if all of them had the same things in their bags, just in case they got separated.

The girls packed the car and drove to where Vitus was hiding out. He had found a vacant house in Gregori's street that he had managed to get into and use to keep tabs on him. Within ten minutes, they arrived just around the corner from the mechanic's house. It was near dusk, and Vitus was standing on the street corner, waiting for them.

"He is still in his house, but we need to be quick; he has been acting strange all day," said Vitus with an urgency to his voice.

The girls got out of the car and tried to discreetly walk down the street to the house. It proved a bit difficult, since they had to put the trank gun in a rucksack. They didn't want to draw attention to themselves, and walking down the street with a gun would definitely turn heads. The gang walked up to Gregori's front door and knocked. Grace felt a bit silly standing on the porch dressed in black and carrying her bags. She looked over at Rose, who was staring at the door intently. There was no answer, so they knocked again but a bit louder. After a few more knocks, there was no answer. Rose performed her little unlocking spell on the door and opened it up. Rhea yelled into the house and walked in. She disappeared inside. Grace could hear her moving about and occasionally yelling. After a moment, they heard some hurried footsteps. Rhea appeared with a worried look on her face. She had something in her hand. She showed it to the group. It was a book on folklore. She ruffled the pages and opened to one that was dog-eared. Grace didn't have her enchanted glasses on her, but she didn't need them to know what it was about. The pictures said it all. There were pictures depicting a werewolf changing.

"I think he saw this and ran," said Rhea.

After some cursing and a foot stamp from Rose, they had to come up with a new plan—and fast. Sunset was fast approaching, and they were running out of time.

"I can track him," said Vitus. He turned and went around the back of the house. He disappeared out of sight and then, after a minute, reappeared around the other side.

"He went out the back door and into the alleyway behind the house." Vitus turned and went into the backyard again. The girls followed closely behind him. Grace was watching Vitus's back; he looked so primal in his movements, and she found it quite fascinating. He sped up, and they ended up in the street. Vitus stopped and looked left and then right. "He went this way."

They took off jogging, heading right. As they were running, Grace took in their surroundings and noticed that they were near the woods.

"He must be heading towards the woods," huffed Grace.

"Look!" Rhea shouted, pointing. A few metres in front

of them was a trail of ripped clothing. "He must have transformed here."

They reached the edge of the woods and stopped.

"He is in there. I can sense it," said Vitus. He sounded a bit tense.

"Are you okay?" asked Grace, sounding concerned.

"Yeah. I'm in hunt mode," he said with a smile.

That made Grace smile. The way he had said it sounded so sexy to her.

"We should pair up and look around," said Rhea. "Rose, go with Grace, and I'll go with Vitus."

Grace made sure that trank gun was loaded and ready to go. When done, she nodded. Vitus walked up to her and gave her a brief kiss. "Be careful."

With that the two parties went in their separate directions. Grace's heart was thundering in her chest, and she felt as if she should be wearing a suit of armour. Rose and Grace waked in a straight line in silence. Grace wasn't sure what was classed as appropriate chatter in situations like this. Rose's eyes were fixed on the ground, as if she was looking for something. Grace thought this odd, since the werewolf would be easily spotted.

"What are you looking for?" Grace asked, hoping to break the silence.

"DNA," Rose answered curtly. She must have been deep in concentration.

Oh yeah, Grace thought to herself, feeling stupid for forgetting. *If Rose gets some DNA, she can track him using her spell!* She instantly started to look around on the ground too, hoping to find something.

After searching and walking for about half an hour, Rose shouted "Yes!"

The sudden outburst scared Grace nearly out of her skin, and she sent a dart into a tree.

"What is it?" Grace asked. Her adrenalin was pumping, and she was starting to shake a bit.

"Fur," said Rose as she reached out to a branch. Grace squinted her eyes and could make out a few strands of hair.

"Is that his?" Grace asked.

"Hope so," said Rose. She didn't sound too convincing.

Rose grabbed the snagged hairs and studied them. "I am going to use these in the tracking spell. They will lead us either to Gregori or a deer."

Grace hoped it would be the former. She wanted this to be over with—and quickly. The longer she was away from Vitus, the more anxious she felt. Rose cleared a spot on the ground and sat down. She put the hairs in her hand and closed her eyes. Grace could feel the air around her vibrate. The more Rose chanted, the more the air thickened. Grace felt a panic attack coming on and started to concentrate on her breathing. Rose was deep in trace when she started to sway. Grace crouched down next to her best friend and looked into her face. She was concerned. Grace had never seen her friend like this before, and she was worried.

"Blood," Rose muttered.

"What?" Grace asked.

"Blood!" Rose responded boldly.

Grace looked around, confused at what her friend was after. She didn't see any blood.

"Knife!" Rose yelled out.

Finally an instruction I can obey, Grace thought. She

reached into Rose's backpack and rummaged around until her hand found the cold blade. She then pulled the knife out and handed it to her friend. Rose kept her eyes closed and grabbed the blade with the hand that was not holding the hairs. She brought up the hand that was holding the hair and opened her palm, ensuring that the hairs stayed on her fingers. Grace watched with unease as Rose dragged the knife edge across the palm of her hand. Rose then rubbed the hairs through the blood while still chanting. A glow emitted from Rose's hand, and a ball of white light rose up. Rose opened her eyes and smiled proudly. "I did it!"

The light started to move to their left. "This will lead us to him," Rose said.

Rose and Grace followed the light through the woods. It was moving slowly at first, and then it started to move more quickly. They weaved in and out of trees as quietly and as quickly as they could, as they didn't want to alert the werewolf first. After walking for about twenty minutes, Grace started to get déjà vu. Grace could have sworn they had been through this part before.

"Hey, Rose. I think I've seen this tree before," Grace said, pointing to a dead tree that had a spooky look to it. Grace remembered looking at it and thinking how it fitted in with the theme of the night.

"You sure?" Rose replied with a confused look on her face.

They kept up their pace. Grace continued to look at the scenery, searching for more familiar landmarks. She looked on the ground and saw some footprints—their own footprints.

"See! We have been here!" Grace said, pointing at the prints.

Rose looked down, and her eyes widened. "Looks like we are not the only ones."

Grace walked up to where she was looking and felt her stomach drop. She was looking at a giant paw print.

"I think we are being hunted," said Rose, her voice shaking.

Grace gripped the trank gun and tried to swallow but found her throat had gone dry. She looked around and tried not to panic. They had stopped long enough that the glowing ball of light had continued on without them.

"What should we do?" asked Grace, not even attempting to keep her voice steady.

"We can either run or wait for the werewolf to find us," replied Rose.

Grace knew which option she preferred. Against her better judgement, Grace mumbled, "I suppose we wait."

"I'll send Rhea a text and get them to come to us."

As Rose was texting, Grace noticed a moving light coming towards them at a rapid rate through the trees.

"Rose …" Grace said, watching the glowing globe closing in.

Rose looked up, and they both stood back as the globe passed between them. They followed its path with their eyes and watched it stop right in front of a mass of dark, matted hair. The werewolf snarled, showing off its long teeth dripping with saliva and a red fluid that Grace suspected to be blood from its latest feed. She hoped that that feed was of the animal variety and not the two-legged human type. Grace froze momentarily and remembered the trank gun she had slung over her shoulder. Trying not to make any sudden movements, Grace grabbed the gun and moved it into position. Rose brought her hands up, a blue light radiating from them. The werewolf got down on his haunches and lunged towards them. Grace could see he was aiming for Rose. Without giving it much thought, Grace hurtled herself towards Rose and knocked her out of the way. Grace had just enough time to see her friend fall safely to the ground before a huge mass of hair and muscle collided with her. Grace felt the ground come up to her as she fell on her stomach, causing the wind to be knocked out of her.

Terrified and sore, Grace tried to get up, but the wolf had her pinned. She felt hot breath on the back of her neck, and then a blinding pain ripped into her shoulder, making her yell out loud. Grace desperately tried to get out from under the wolf, but it was too big and too strong. Beyond the sound the werewolf was making while tearing into her flesh, Grace heard another growl coming from her right and prayed it wasn't another wolf coming to join the feast. Some thundering footsteps came running in close, and then she felt the wolf get ripped off of her. Using the opportunity, Grace leapt up, ran behind the nearest tree, and braced herself against it. After a few quick breaths, she chanced a glance around it to see what was happening. All she could see was a flurry of fur and another human. It took her a few moments to realize that it was Vitus wrestling with the wolf. There was no sign of Rhea, and Rose was sprawled on the ground with her eyes closed. Grace felt a lump in her throat but noticed that Rose was still breathing. She surmised she must have hit her head when Grace pushed her away.

Cursing under her breath, Grace looked around for

something that could help. A few metres in front of her, she spotted the trank gun lying on the ground. She quickly raced forward, picked up the gun, and took aim. She had to really concentrate to make sure she hit fur and not Vitus's skin. Her shoulder was roaring with pain, but she ignored it and pulled the trigger. She sighed with relief on seeing she had made a direct hit. It didn't take long until the werewolf started to slow down. Vitus untangled himself from the wolf and stood back while it fell into a heap. Grace finally let the gun fall from her hand. A noise from behind her made her jump. She turned around and saw Rhea approaching. Her eyes were wide with shock, and her hair was dishevelled from running

"I'm so sorry. Vitus just took off, and it took me a while to catch up. What happened?" she said while looking around.

Grace wanted to fill her in, but her first priority was Rose. She crouched next to her unconscious friend and checked her out. From what she could tell, all her vitals were fine; they would just have to wait for her to wake up. Unlike Grace, Rose healed at the normal human rate.

Grace stood up and winced. Her shoulder was in agony, and she could feel blood seeping down her back. Vitus walked up to her and looked at the shoulder.

"It's just a bit sore. It will heal," said Grace.

"I don't doubt that, but you were bitten by a werewolf; that's how the curse is transmitted," replied Vitus grimly.

Shit, thought Grace.

CHAPTER 10

Vitus made short work of chaining and securing the werewolf. Grace had to remind him that even though he had bitten her and there was a chance she could be cursed, he had to be gentle when handling him. Vitus's mouth turned into a line when she said that, but he nodded and said he would treat the wolf as if he were porcelain. That made Grace happy. The wolf was still a person, after all. Rose was still unconscious by the time they were ready to move, so Rhea cast a spell on Rose to make her lighter so she could carry her. Grace led the way through the woods. She was still shaking from being bitten and didn't want the others to see the worried look on her face. When they got to the car, they faced another dilemma—how to fit an oversize wolf in Rhea's small car. After much manoeuvring and a few pulled muscles, they managed to fit everyone in the car. Grace was in the front with Rose on her lap, and poor Vitus was crammed in the back with Gregori the wolf. With every bump, Grace felt her shoulder throb. She really wished the healing process were a bit quicker. She never liked pain, and she was pretty sure she was getting blood on Rhea's car seats.

When they got back to Rhea's house, they put Rose's unconscious body into her bed. Grace was going to check up on her later, but first she wanted to make sure the werewolf was properly secured. She went to the basement and saw that Vitus was checking the restraints. It was sad to see the poor animal chained up, but it was for the best. Once Vitus finished his checks, he looked up at Grace with concern in his eyes. "He isn't going anywhere. Let's go upstairs and have a look at that bite."

Grace nodded. She wasn't quite sure what to say. She could put a brave face on in front of the girls, but not Vitus.

They walked upstairs and sat in the kitchen. The lighting was better there. Vitus carefully peeled Grace's bloodied shirt from her shoulder. It stung, but Grace held her tongue.

"How does it look?" asked Grace, her voice breaking.

"Doesn't look like it's started to heal yet," Vitus replied tensly.

Grace's heart dropped. She healed at a rapid rate, and she knew that if she hadn't healed by now, something must be wrong.

"The bite must have been deep," Grace said, trying to convince herself more than Vitus.

They sat in silence while Vitus cleaned and dressed the wound. He was just putting the last bit of tape on when Rhea walked in and sat opposite them. "Rose is awake. She said she feels okay and is having a shower. I filled her in on what happened."

"Is she mad at me?" Grace asked, hoping she wasn't.

"She tried to be, but you know Rose; she can't stay mad very long," replied Rhea.

"I will talk to her in the morning. Right now I feel like a warm bath and a long sleep," said Grace.

"I will stay up and look after Gregori. We need to keep him sedated until he turns back into his human form," said Vitus, getting up from his seat. "Do you need a hand, dear Grace?"

"No, I can handle it," replied Grace. She wanted to be alone so she could process the night's events.

"Okay, I shall be in the basement if you require anything." With that, he gave Grace's hand a squeeze and headed downstairs.

"Are you okay? You don't need to act brave around me," said Rhea.

"I am fine, just tired and sore. I will see you in the morning." Grace got up and went to her room. She barely made it to her door before the first tear fell. She had no idea what she would do if she became a werewolf.

The next morning, Grace was woken up by a knock on her door.

"Come in," she said in answer.

The door opened, and Grace sat up, rubbing the sleep from her eyes.

"You are such an idiot," said a voice.

"Love you too, Rose," said Grace.

Rose turned on the bedroom light, and Grace's eyes screamed in protest.

"Agh!" said Grace, blinking.

Rose stood next to Grace's bed with her hands on her hips. "What did you go and get yourself bitten for!"

"Didn't want you to get hurt," mumbled Grace through the sleep.

"I would have been fine. You didn't need to go all martyr on me," replied Rose.

"Rose, you are my best friend. If I had to cut off my arm and throw it into the woods to distract that wolf, I would have," Grace said.

Rose leapt onto the bed and wrapped her arms around Grace. "You are so stupid sometimes, but I love you dearly. Don't do that again."

Grace hugged her friend back. "Hopefully I won't have to."

"Let me have a look at this bite," said Rose.

Grace turned her back to her friend and felt her shirt get lifted up.

"I am going to take the dressing off, and I am not going to be gentle about it," said Rose.

Grace laughed and gritted her teeth as she felt the dressing slowly being removed. She heard Rose gasp when she had fully taken it off.

"It's still there and fresh, huh?" replied Grace.

"Yeah," said Rose sadly. "It is."

This was the longest Grace had ever had a fresh wound, and she was starting to feel anxious.

Rose re-dressed the bite, and they made their way to the kitchen to get breakfast and to see what had happened overnight with Gregori. They were quite surprised when they saw him sitting at the kitchen table, staring into his coffee. Rhea was sitting next to him. She looked up as they walked into the room. She said something to Gregori, who just nodded, and she got up and motioned for the girls to follow her. Rhea led them out into the hallway. Vitus was still asleep in the lounge.

"How is he?" asked Grace.

"Well, he finally believes us," replied Rhea. "He said that after we left the office, he couldn't stop thinking about what we had said and how much of it made sense. He then started to do some research. When he realized what we said was true, he panicked and had to get out of the house to get some air, but he didn't realize it was a full moon until he noticed the signs of his change approaching."

"Did he say what those signs were?" Grace asked, as she wanted to know what to look out for.

"He said that first he felt really hot; then his senses became sharper—more defined. Following that, he got a sharp pain is his head, and his whole body vibrated. The last thing he remembers before he changed is his heart rate changing rapidly. Then he recalls nothing until he woke up back in human form."

"So you mean he doesn't remember biting Grace?" Rose asked.

"He doesn't, but we told him reluctantly. He could tell Vitus was upset at him for something, so he got it out of us eventually. He is very upset about it and wants to find a way to apologize," said Rhea.

"It's not his fault," said Grace sympathetically. "Come; let's go meet him." She was determined to show Gregori that there were no hard feelings, no matter what the outcome was.

The girls walked back into the kitchen. Grace sat opposite Gregori. He glanced up with the saddest look on his face. He started to talk, and Rhea translated.

"He said he is so sorry he has bitten you. He said he

should have listened to us and wants to make it up to you any way he can," said Rhea.

Grace smiled at Gregori. "Please tell him that it's okay. He didn't do it on purpose. If I turn, then I can deal with it. It's not the worst thing that has ever happened to me."

Rhea translated what Grace said. When she finished, Gregori had a puzzled look on his face. He asked a question of Rhea, who answered back without translating to Grace. They exchanged a bit of back-and-forth, and the only name Grace could make out was "Solomon." She knew Rhea must be telling him about the sorcerer.

"He wants to help you," said Rhea.

Grace had stopped listening while they were talking "Pardon?"

"He said he feels bad and wants to help. He said he will quit his job and accompany you to find Solomon," Rhea said.

"Oh, I can't accept that. What about his family? Surely they will miss him?"

Rhea exchanged some words with Gregori. "He said that he hasn't got any family. He was adopted at a young age, and his adoptive parents died years ago. He asks that you please let him help you. He hasn't got much of a life here, and since he now knows what is happening to him, he doesn't want to be around normal humans until he knows what being a werewolf is about. He thinks we can help him with that."

Grace saw the sense in that. "Okay, but he isn't bound to us. He can leave whenever he wants."

After Rhea translated, Gregori nodded and held out his hand, and Grace shook it.

He said something else to Rhea, which she translated. "He said he had better learn English then."

That night they helped Gregori chain himself up in Rhea's basement. When they were finished, Vitus grabbed Grace's hand and turned to lead her upstairs. Grace stopped and let go of his hand. "If you don't mind, I would like to see him change so I know what to expect."

Rhea translated, and Gregori nodded. Grace sat herself against a wall. Within moments, Vitus joined her. "You won't have to go through this alone."

Grace smiled and leaned her head against his shoulder. She was thankful that he decided to stay with her.

Time ticked by slowly, and Gregori started to change about two hours after sundown. It looked horrific. First he started to groan, and then he began panting. Grace watched with a mixture of fascination and horror and the man's skin started to crawl. He gave a sharp yell as each of his limbs started to morph into a more doglike shape. Another scream sounded, and the skin seemed to split off Gregori's back. Underneath it looked like wet fur. One big growl radiated from the beast, and with one lurch, the skin disappeared and the form of the wolf took over. The wolf shook and looked towards Vitus and Grace. Vitus got up and grabbed the tranquillizer gun on the ground next to him. Grace was impressed that he remembered it. He took aim and shot the werewolf. It was a direct hit. The wolf growled and snapped in their direction; then he started to sway on his feet. It didn't take too much longer before the werewolf was lying on the floor, sleeping. Grace released the breath that she had been holding; she hoped she would never have to experience that.

The following month, Grace was preparing herself for the worst. The wound had finally healed after two weeks. That worried everyone. Grace kept a brave face on when with the others, but when she was alone, she let the panic consume her. They had a cage ready for Gregori, along with plenty of tranquillizers for him. They decided to just chain Grace up and observe her. If she changed, they would get a cage the next day. Grace was sitting on her bed, counting down the seconds before she had to go down to the basement. A knock on the door indicated that it was time. Grace stood up and opened the door. Vitus was standing there with a worried look on his face. "Ready?" he asked.

"Yeah" was all Grace could croak out.

They walked into the basement hand in hand.

Gregori was already sitting in his cage. "Hello," he said. He looked sad as they walked into the room. Over the last month, Rhea had been teaching him English. They could now have short conversations, and he had a pretty good sense of humour too.

Grace smiled, hoping to reassure Gregori. "Hello" was all she could manage.

Rose came down too. "We will be right here with you."

"Thank you, but no need. I would rather it be just me and Vitus."

Vitus squeezed her hand.

"Are you sure?" asked Rose.

"Yes," replied Grace.

"Okay, I have some things I need to work on anyway," said Rose unconvincingly.

Grace hoped that these things were related to Solomon. Now that they had helped Rhea, she was in full swing, helping them look for the witch coven they had heard about.

When Rose left, Grace stood in position and Vitus

helped her with her chains. They were heavy and cold. Once she was all chained and secured, Grace found that she had to sit down under the weight of the chains. Vitus leaned down and kissed her head; then he walked over to the wall, tranquillizer gun in hand.

The silence was deafening as they waited. A moaning drew Grace's attention to Gregori, who was starting his change. Grace turned her head and stared at Vitus, who was looking at Grace. They held the stare until a roar came from the werewolf. Vitus's eyes shifted as he took aim and tranquillized the wolf. As soon as the dart stuck, he looked at Grace again. Minutes ticked by, and there was still no change. Grace looked over at the sleeping mound that was Gregori. After a few hours went by, Grace started to get tired. Vitus must have realized how tired she was, and he gave her a pillow.

"Thanks," Grace said. She wasn't sure how, but she drifted off to sleep.

A rustling sound woke Grace up. She sat up and noticed that Vitus had removed the chains while she was asleep.

"You looked uncomfortable," she heard Vitus say from across the room. His face looked solemn.

"Did I …?" Grace started.

A smile broke out across Vitus's face. He didn't need to say anything.

"Yes!" Grace yelled. Then she quickly covered her mouth, remembering that there was a slumbering wolf in the same room.

Vitus laughed. "It's okay. He won't wake any time soon."

Grace got up and went over to Vitus, and they embraced.

"I am so relieved. I am honestly not sure how I would have been able to handle being an immortal werewolf," said Grace.

"You would have been fine. I believe in you," said Vitus, looking deeply into Grace's eyes.

Grace smiled and wrapped her arms around Vitus's neck and brought him in for a kiss. The kiss was so passionate; it was the celebration that Grace needed.

"Let's go upstairs and tell the others," said Grace.

"If they are still awake. It's three in the morning," replied Vitus.

They walked into the kitchen, where Rose was hunched over her laptop. She squealed when she saw Grace emerge from the steps. "I thought you would be okay! One curse must be enough for one person." She came over and hugged Grace. "I am really happy you are okay. If you turned into a werewolf trying to save me, I would have killed you."

Grace smiled. "Good thing I am immortal."

"I have more good news. I have a good lead on this coven. Rhea has a friend that met with one of the members in England. She reckons that she can organize a meet-and-greet."

Grace's heart thundered in her chest. They were finally getting somewhere; she was finally going to get her revenge. But first things first.

"As much as I really want to meet them, I want to put a stop to Dr. Werner first," said Grace.

"I agree. We will put together a letter to get passed on. In the meantime, we can deal with the doctor and his facility."

Pleased with the outcome, Grace felt relief wash over

her. Everything was starting to fall into place. She yawned and realized how tired she actually was.

"You should go to bed," said Rose.

"And you. You looked tired," replied Grace.

"I will. I'm just checking a few things out; then I am going to bed too."

"Okay, good night," said Grace as she hugged her friend.

"Good night," replied Rose.

Vitus grabbed Grace's hand and walked her to her bedroom. He gave her a kiss and turned to leave, but Grace held his hand tighter.

"Would you like to come in?" Grace asked, her palms sweating with nerves.

Vitus gave her a look and said, "Are you sure?"

"I have never been so sure in my life," Grace breathed.

Vitus smiled, and they walked into the bedroom. Grace was smiling broadly in the dark as she felt for the light switch. She couldn't think of a better night to take the next step in their relationship. Grace found the switch and turned it on. What she saw on the bed made the colour drain from her face "Oh no," she said, stumbling towards the thing that had caused all feelings of passion to leave her.

"What is it?" Vitus asked confusedly.

Grace stood up and showed him what was in her hand. It was a beautiful peacock feather.

"He knows," Grace said grimly. "Solomon knows we are searching for him."

Printed in the United States
By Bookmasters